# COMMUNITY GARDEN

## BY KYLA STAN

Copyright 2025 by Kyla Stan
All rights reserved.
Bakersfield font and images by Nikki Laatz of Creative Market
Cover design by Margaux G. on Fiverr

This ebook, illustrations or any portion thereof may not be reproduced or used in any manner whatsoever including information storage and retrieval systems, without permission in writing from the author except for the use of brief quotations in a book review. This ebook may not be re-sold or given away to other people. If you would like to share this ebook with another person, please purchase an additional copy for each recipient.

This ebook is a work of fiction. Names, characters, places, and incidents either are products of the author's imagination or are used fictitiously. Any resemblance to actual persons, living or dead, events, or locales is entirely coincidental.

# OTHER BOOKS BY THE AUTHOR

**The Skin Walker Series**
*A teenage Goth girl is accidentally bitten by a werewolf, setting off an ancient prophecy. With high fantasy elements and reference to Native American myths, this is the book that started the author's writing journey (final book coming soon!)*

**Forbidden Tides: A Dark YA Mermaid Romance**
*Some would say I look like a mermaid, the essence of nautical beauty. I looked in the mirror and saw a monster.... Astrid Murphy constantly craves the salty Californian ocean and her strange webbed hands disgust her father. When a merman washes up on shore, she learns about her true nature and what it means to be free*

**Nightshade: Poems of Heartbreak, Love, and Lust**
*A collection of Gothic-inspired poetry divided into six topics: heartbreak, love, the mind, nature, story poems, and poems inspired by Poet Tongue, the first novel in The Skin Walker series.*

**Ocean Song: Stories of Mermaids, Selkies, and Underwater Mysteries**
Travel to uncharted cities, meet feral mermaids, and discover undersea mysteries in this anthology of short stories and poems. Described by beta readers as "a love letter to the ocean," Kyla Stan explores the turbulent relationship between humans and the ocean, representing varied emotions from grief to fear to seduction.

**Femme Fatale: Horror Stories With Dangerous Women**
In this newest collection by Kyla Stan, each story explores the concept of femme fatale through a variety of fanged and furious creatures. From ancient witches to vengeful ghosts, each woman in the story uses her beauty and seductive powers to lure her target into their clutches.

THIS IS WHAT NUYORICAN CULTURE IS ABOUT. IT DOESN'T MATTER WHAT SKIN COLOR YOU'RE BORN WITH, WHETHER YOU'RE STRAIGHT OR GAY OR IF YOU SPEAK FLUENT SPANISH. BORICUA LIFE IS ABOUT FAMILY: SHARING YOUR LOVE, PAIN, AND EXPERIENCES, THEN FINDING COMMON GROUND OVER THE DINNER TABLE.

TO ALL WHO SUFFER IN SILENCE: I SEE YOU, HEAR YOUR STORY, AND HOPE THESE WORDS SPEAK YOUR TRUTH.

# TABLE OF CONTENTS

| | |
|---|---|
| OTHER BOOKS BY THE AUTHOR | 3 |
| TABLE OF CONTENTS | 5 |
| PROLOGUE | 6 |
| CHAPTER 1: MAMI SAYS | 7 |
| CHAPTER 2: PORQUE PAPI | 9 |
| CHAPTER 3: BRUJA SECRETA | 11 |
| CHAPTER 4: THE ANNOUNCEMENT | 15 |
| CHAPTER 5: LAS CHISPAS | 20 |
| CHAPTER 6: AMOR? | 23 |
| CHAPTER 7: PASTELITOS | 27 |
| CHAPTER 8: AZUCAR! | 32 |
| CHAPTER 9: TIAS Y TIOS | 38 |
| CHAPTER 10: MIGUEL'S PROMISE | 39 |
| CHAPTER 11: THE CLEANUP | 41 |
| CHAPTER 12: FIERY FLARE | 45 |
| CHAPTER 13: CARNIVAL THRILLS | 48 |
| CHAPTER 14: THE FIRST SEEDS | 53 |
| CHAPTER 15: EL PLANTON | 59 |
| CHAPTER 16: FUEGO | 62 |
| CHAPTER 17: MY "PERFECT" FAMILY | 64 |
| CHAPTER 18: NUESTRO CORAZONES | 66 |
| CHAPTER 19: PAPI'S MEMORY | 69 |
| CHAPTER 20: MY FUTURE | 70 |
| EPILOGUE | 73 |
| AUTHOR'S NOTE | 75 |
| THE SKIN WALKER SERIES BOOK 1 | 77 |
| FORBIDDEN TIDES: A DARK YA MERMAID ROMANCE | 78 |
| STAY CONNECTED WITH THE AUTHOR! | 79 |

# PROLOGUE

Sunlight filters through my bedroom window, but my computer screen is blank, a teasing reminder that time is almost up. Despite the open window and old air conditioner, the air is stifling, and I take a deep breath while wiping my brow. I rub my temples and close my eyes, begging the first words of my story to write themselves. Outside, the birds sing of sweet freedom that I desire before heading off to college. I *have* to get this done. I bite my lip and start writing. *When my papi died, I didn't know what to do.* I sigh in frustration and delete the sentence. Clearly, I'm having a case of fibromyalgia brain fog, but I also crave the ocean's roar and salty breezes. It doesn't help that my thrift store desk is cluttered with college applications, photos of Jayden and Nolia…of Papi. His absence pierces my heart.

Downstairs, my family watches a TV game show with luxurious prize packages, and I envy them. I desperately want to relax and enjoy my summer. Grandma's cackling laugh startles me, and I close my eyes. My hands ball into fists and I try not to scream, throwing my head back with an exasperated sigh. When my long black curls become a frizzled mess, I tie my hair into a neat ponytail, then try to compose myself.

I've been working on this essay for a week, starting a sentence or paragraph and then deleting everything. My senior project essay is due tonight, and I thought I would've finished by now. I tap my pencil against the computer screen and look outside. I consider the last few months, my silent promise to Papi that I would follow through on my project and move past his death to find my purpose.

*Think of the garden, Nichi. The greenery, floral smells, and your hard work.*

But when did this all happen? When did my neurons fire this *chispa* of an idea?

My brown eyes ignite with determination, and I hear his encouraging voice in my head. *You can do this, baby. Just breathe and focus.*

My hands fly over the keyboard, the words flowing like a cathartic release, and I don't stop myself this time.

# CHAPTER 1: MAMI SAYS

*I'll never forget the day I woke up and every joint in my body screamed in pain, crushed by some unknown force. A month after Papi died, my body attacked itself, and everything changed.*

I leaned my head against the cool window and appreciated that it was January, right after Christmas. Leftover lights twinkled among thick icicles, and snow drifts warmed my heart.

Winter is the only season that eases the pain in my joints and prevents massive flares.

But the window was closed, and I would've gotten smacked if I opened it. As we drove over the Verrazano and headed back into my hood, Mami drummed her fingers on the steering wheel to salsa music from the radio. "So, *mija*," her voice was tense; I had to *escuchar*, to listen carefully. But my head slumped against the window, and I internally groaned. Mami had blasted the car heater, and I fried like a plantain in screaming oil.

*¡Nichi, escúchame!"*

I shook my head and tossed my black, sweaty curls behind me, and rubbed my eyes. "Sorry."

Mami sighed long and hard, full of Puerto Rican spitfire and impatience.

"The doctor said to push through, Nilsa, especially when you're exhausted."

I rolled my eyes. "Yeah, Mami. I get it. Push through like it doesn't exist."

"Nichi, you cannot let your disability get the best of you. If Papi were still alive—"

"Stop. We're not talking about this. Not now."

Mami pressed her glossed lips in a thin line and turned her attention back to the radio.

I gritted my teeth and stared outside at the geometric shapes all colliding for attention across New York City. I'm a Nuyorican, a girl born in the city with deep Puerto Rican roots, but we don't live in the shiny parts where all the rich ladies show off their designer purses and toy dogs. We live in the Bronx, a gritty, beautiful slice of Puerto Rican culture. I realized Mami was talking about something else, and I hadn't responded.

"Are you listening?"

"Not really."

Mami pinched the bridge of her nose. I turned to study her, light caramel skin always ablaze in makeup, hair curled to perfection even for a trip to the doctor's office on Long Island. Mami always said, "dress like you're meeting a movie star and not like *basura*," or garbage. "Put effort into yourself, no matter the cost."

When Mami and Grandma had emigrated from Puerto Rico, people treated her like dirty foreigners, as if she didn't belong in America even though *la isla* is a part of the States. They had worked their asses off just to get a decent apartment. Now, Mami works as a manager in a hotel on Park Avenue, and Grandma is retired.

"Women in our Rivera family are strong, Nilsa, resilient, and even a little magical." She smiled, hinting at the days our ancestors performed Santería, an ancient voodoo magic considered taboo. "Stop letting your flares get the best of you, okay?"

I opened my mouth but snapped it shut, staring out the window as we passed over rough roads and headed to the pharmacy. Mami parked the car near "La Pharmacia Grande" in our hood and asked if I wanted anything.

I smirk. "Just a chocolate bar."

She rolled her eyes and gave me a warning look. "Okay, sure. If you want to keep gaining weight." Her heels clicked on the pavement as she hurried inside to pick up my five prescriptions.

Five. All for pain, to tell my nerves to chill the hell out.

I pinched my lower belly and leaned on the window, trying not to let her words get to me. But Mami says,

"You never push past your pain."

"You're lazy."

"You sleep too much."

*"¡Qué gordita, Nilsa!"*

My eyes drifted shut to catch a moment of rest, but her comments buzzed in my mind like angry hornets. I had explained this before, but the conversation goes in circles.

Does she believe a seventeen-year-old wants to feel like a decrepit?

I sighed and thought of Papi's smile.

## CHAPTER 2: PORQUE PAPI

Papi, known as Chip Sandford by those in my community, was the local fix-it guy. Papi was a gringo, and before he was accepted into our Nuyorican community, people had judged him. But when they watched his magic hands fix anything and everything, and how he wasn't another racist who chanted, "go back to your country," they accepted him. Growing up, we never hired mechanics *porque* Papi learned it all. But Papi had his vices and never took care of himself. The doctor had warned he was born with a birth defect in his heart, and he was lucky to be alive.

But Papi said it was up to God.

And I never thought He would turn his back on us.

It had been a perfect summer Saturday. The window was open, letting in the humid air and an artificial floral scent from our downstairs neighbor's detergent. Our entire family relaxed in the crowded living room, listening to a telenovela. Papi had a beer in hand, and my siblings played on the floor with their toys while Mami crocheted a blanket for Grandma. With a startled gasp, I watched Papi spew his beer and clutch his chest. He fell on his knees, let out a hoarse scream, and threw up.

Within minutes, we rushed into an ambulance by his side while his face turned pale and ashen. The *beep, beep… beep…* of the vitals monitor faded. Within an hour, he was dead. We didn't get to say goodbye or hold his hand because nurses and cardiologists swarmed over him.

"A blot clot," the doctor said, "blocked his artery."

I fell to the floor alongside Mami and Grandma, their howling cries drowning my emotions. Like a skipping video, I remember his brief last moments, but my mind always locks onto his terrible, painful scream. The words repeated in my head. *He's dead. Papi is dead.*

All within one hour.

Papi's funeral was humble but filled with people who truly loved and appreciated him.

*Porque* Papi is dead, I live with constant pain in my joints and I'm always exhausted, even when I take my medicine. Fibromyalgia constantly haunts every waking moment of my life, a reminder of my trauma and why my body goes into overdrive.

*Porque* Papi, I've lost all hope that I'll never return to normal.

*Y porque* Papi, my life has been a constant reminder that my father, the one who never judged me, allowed me to make my own decisions, and thought I was beautiful, *not gordita,* is gone forever.

# CHAPTER 3: BRUJA SECRETA

When we arrived home, my body ached with flu-like pains despite the nerve medication in my system. I silently prayed this flare wouldn't last too long; I still had an essay to work on. Outside, the bitter cold soothed my pain, and I breathed in the distant scent of fireplace smoke, a single trace of the holidays. I stared past my barrio as the sky dimmed into winter grays and frosted pinks.

Mami playfully swatted my butt and ushered me inside. When the door opened, my senses went into overdrive. Grandma had almost finished cooking, and I smelled my favorite: paella with fresh shellfish! I smiled while she stirred the big pot and giggled at my grumbling stomach. "Hi Grandma!"

*"¡Hola, mija!"* She shuffled over in her tattered slippers to give me a gentle kiss and hug. Her caramel skin matches my mother's, but her hair is like a white cloud of frizzed curls. Mami hung up her thick winter coat and purse before setting the table. Even if I wanted to, I can't help. The kitchen was cramped and chaotic with just Mami and Grandma. Instead, I seated myself at the aging table and watched the scene through the open kitchen.

"Time for dinner!" Mami calls upstairs.

"Mami! You're home!" Willie, my eight-year-old brother, screamed while charging down the steps. Isabela sauntered down in her Disney princess gown. Her sassy five-year-old ways made me grin. They both gave me a kiss and sat down across the table.

Grandma placed the paella in the middle of the table, and all three of us salivated, waiting to finish our daily prayer. Mami sat at the head of the table and signaled for us to join hands. In Spanish she said, "God, thank you for the food we are about to eat. Thank you for our happiness, prosperity (I try not to scoff at this one), and health (more mental scoffing.) We pray for others less fortunate than us, and we pray for peace. Amen."

"Amen," Grandma, Willie, and Isabela mimicked.

I couldn't finish the prayer nor accept the words, but I bowed my head, so Mami didn't flip out. Everyone's eyes briefly locked on Papi's chair.

Nobody dared touch it, a silent memorial that was sacred. Then we transitioned to normal conversation like he had never existed. I lowered my eyes and focused on the plate. Grandma served us a generous helping, then passed me the hot sauce and winked. She knows I can't have one meal without it.

"So, how did the doctor's visit go, Nichi?"

Mami sighed. "Well, she's not *better*, and the doctor put her on more gabapentin plus something else to help with the pain."

I shuffled the clamshells around, their *clinking* filling the silence in the room. Grandma ignored Mami and glanced at me over her glasses.

"It went okay, I guess. I mean, it could be worse, right? I could have something like rheumatoid arthritis."

"That's my girl. Always positive." Grandma patted my hand. The conversation turned to Isi and Willie as they recounted their school day.

"I learned about Columbus!" Willie yelled and raised his hand.

Isi smiled. "I shared my toys and snack with the new girl."

I nodded at them and smiled while digging into a mussel with my fork.

"That's great, Willie. I'm glad you paid attention. And Isi, that's wonderful!" Mami smiled. Grandma kept them occupied with conversation while I finished dinner. She has a sixth sense when my fibromyalgia is bothering me, but unlike Mami, she doesn't shame me for it.

When we finished dinner, I helped Grandma with the plates and put the leftovers away. "*¡Gracias, mija!* I really need a break from standing." Grandma muttered "*coño,*" under her breath and shuffled into the living room to watch her shows with Mami. Grandma has degenerative hip disease, which means her bones are disintegrating, so even when I flare, I always help. And for those of you new to Spanish, that's one of the worst curse words. I stifled a giggle at her cursing and pulled out some foil to cover the paella before heading upstairs to finish my essay.

As I trudged upstairs, I heard Willie and Isi playing with their toys before Mami came upstairs to get them ready for bed. Her room is on the right. Grandma used to have her own room, but now we use it to store Papi's stuff. Mami couldn't stand sleeping alone, so Grandma shared a bed with her. My room is the last down the hall, and I welcomed the sweet relief of comfy yoga pants and a baggy t-shirt before jumping on my bed. I grabbed my laptop but stopped when I noticed my reflection in the vanity mirror.

I have Mami's unruly black curls and chocolate eyes, but my skin is pale, the same as Papi's; the only feature I inherited from him. I smile. He had used to joke that Mami's genes are bossy and took over the rest of my body. In my neighborhood, white skin can get you into trouble. Thankfully, I'm fluent in Spanish and people around here know Mami and Grandma. But it raised the question: am I Boricua enough? Papi's skin tone will live with me forever, but do I need to be caramel skinned like Grandma and Mami for acceptance? I folded my thoughts away like old parchment and turned on my laptop.

The essay's topic: Productivity on Winter Break.

The answer: difficult to be truthful. Should I have explained that my flares became worse? That my body constantly felt like it was fighting the flu, my bones splitting every time I moved? How basic tasks had become difficult, and I was scared? I pushed my laptop aside and cried into my pillow so Grandma and Mami didn't hear. But without it, my sobs would've been gut-wrenching, full of frustration and torture. Mami thought I was lazy or in shock from Papi dying. Grandma pitied me, and my siblings didn't know what had happened to their father. I wiped my eyes and rinsed my face with cold water in the bathroom. Then I took a deep breath and resumed my essay.

*Over winter break, I learned that productivity means constantly helping around the house, no matter the cost.*

Toward eleven-thirty, I heard Grandma shuffle upstairs and shut off the lights. She's the last one to sleep since she loves playing on her tablet and watching TV. When everyone fell asleep and my essay was finished, I took a deep breath and headed toward the back of my closet. Tucked among old clothes, stuffed animals, and mementos was my altar to Gaia. She is the voice and mother of Earth, femininity, a solid answer to the positive and negative aspects of life.

I wanted to light a white and blue candle, one for purity and one for health. Hell, I wish I could've lit a bunch of colors, but since my altar was tucked away, I didn't want to start a fire. I envisioned the flames and sensed its gentle warmth. I even inhaled a small jar of incense for psychic clarity. Once I felt grounded, I turned my gaze toward Gaia. I have never felt judged for past mistakes or missing a prayer. Her green skin and swollen belly resembled the earth and were a welcoming sight. She will always accept me, flaws and all.

I closed my eyes.

"Goddess Gaia, tonight I come asking for healing, both in my heart and mind. I know I have come to you with this blessing request before, and I know you will show me a way, but please—" I choked back my tears. "I need to feel whole again, to have a purpose in my life." I stopped and listened for the stealthy steps of Mami or if I sensed a message from the Goddess. There was a strange warmth in my core, a feeling of connectivity to a higher spirit.

"Thank you, Goddess. Blessed Be."

I made the sign of the pentagram by touching my forehead, two points on my chest, and two points on my shoulders. I yawned and headed into bed, then lied awake for a while, considering the universe and if someone had listened. In a Boricua household, *Dios* is always watching, but he's also always *judging*. I had stayed in the "broom closet," a reference to those who practice in secret because I didn't want my family to say I worshipped the devil.

But I don't, and my spirituality is about peace and acceptance.

So why should I worship someone who judges me like Mami?

# CHAPTER 4: THE ANNOUNCEMENT

The next morning, Mami rushed to work as usual. She slammed one of the vanity drawers in the bathroom and blasted the blow dryer. So, I woke up at five-thirty alongside her and poured some cereal. My eyes felt glued shut even though I washed my face with ice-cold water. I groaned and rubbed my face, desperate to crawl back under my sheets. In the bedroom, Grandma snored like an old cow, peacefully unaware of our hectic household. She always sleeps in and takes the kids to pre-K. Otherwise, I'm alone in the mornings.

Before I headed to school, I poured myself an extra strong cup of café Bustelo and inhaled the rich, bitter aroma. I added a little sugar and cream in the thermos, grabbed my bag, and unlocked the door. My best friend Nolia waited on the steps with earbuds blasting a dubstep beat. Her full name is Magnolia, like the beautiful Southern flower, but she prefers a shortened version because her full name sounds too old-fashioned. "Like *un nombre de vieja!*" she had shouted when we were children.

"Hey, girl." Nolia smiled.

I sighed. "Hi."

"Don't worry. The exercise will do you good, remember?"

"Mhm." More advice from the doctor echoed by someone else.

We walked in silence, and I studied Nolia. She's my Dominican sister from another island, with dark chocolate skin and lush braids. I was jealous of her ethnic beauty and felt like a confusion of features.

As we passed through *el barrio*, we waved to Mr. Jimenez, the corner store owner, and the ladies leaving their apartments for work. The rush of traffic and honking cars invaded our Burrough like concrete jungle birds. Otherwise, everything was gray and muddled from the dirty snow drifts.

Nolia put her phone and earbuds away. "How was your doctor's appointment?"

I rolled my eyes, and my mouth puckered like I swallowed a lemon. "Good. I guess."

She smiled and nuzzled my shoulder. People with fibromyalgia have areas called "tender points" where pain is at its highest. My shoulders screamed with a deep ache. "Come on, you can tell me."

I told her how the doctor had increased my medicine and how Mami busted my hump about pushing through the pain. She will never understand my struggles, but I always appreciate that she's willing to listen.

At the school's entrance, a few kids and faculty stood outside, most with a warm cup of coffee or hot chocolate. I ignored the chatter and focused on Nolia. "Did you finish the winter break essay?"

She chuckled. "Barely. I finished it last night."

"Me too," I grinned. "But what's next?"

She pursed her lips. "Homeroom teachers are probably going to discuss senior project."

"Hopefully it's just another boring ass essay, and that's it."

The bell rang and we split up, promising to meet for lunch like always. Even though it was seven forty-five, everyone was loud as hell like they drank an entire pot of coffee with Adderall.

Just before I reached my locker, I stopped short. Talia, my arch enemy since third grade, stood close to my homeroom door, and when she noticed me, her grin widened like a predator.

"Well, well. Look who survived winter break!" Talia announced. Her heels clacked closer to me with her two "friends" by her side. Back in third grade, I had corrected Talia on a geography question, and she instantly made me public enemy number one. But nowadays, she targeted my weight with cruel accuracy. Even in the frigid weather, she wore a miniskirt and a low-cut blouse. Oh, and her signature glittery barrette. She tossed her pin-straight auburn hair over her shoulder and crossed her arms.

I opened my locker and grabbed my books. "Get lost, Talia."

"Or what? You're gonna cry like you did in the gym locker room?" She slapped my books out of my hands and cackled down the hallway. I sighed and rolled my eyes, then grabbed my stuff. The only reason Nolia and I didn't fight Talia was our Spanish don't-ever-get-in-trouble moms. They didn't tolerate that ghetto bullshit. Ever since I became her target, there was a subtle shift in the way people looked at me, some with pity and others like I was cursed. Nobody wanted to cross Talia and become an ostracized loser.

I slammed my locker and sulked into homeroom.

Mrs. Perez looked up from her desk. "Good morning, Nichi. How are you today?"

"Hey Mrs. Perez. Same old, nothing new."

Mrs. Perez had been notified of my health struggles for the past few months. Usually, teachers didn't allow students to eat or drink in the classrooms, but she knew coffee helped me get through the day. She wasn't the average glasses-and-geek kind of teacher. Oh *no*; she's the definition of a Latina super model, with long black hair and intense curves. I still don't understand why she works in our school instead of gracing magazine covers.

Only a few kids sat in homeroom, and I sipped my coffee in silence. I scrolled through social media on my phone for fifteen minutes before the warning bell blared through the hallways. Everyone trudged inside and plopped down, some still bleary-eyed while others were wide awake.

Mrs. Perez took attendance, then moved to the front of the classroom. "Okay everyone, quiet down! Alicia, put your phone away for the millionth time. Clara and Bobby, enough." She paused and waited for the room to shut up. "As you know, we are halfway through your final year, and it's time to brainstorm ideas for your senior project." A united groan sounded through the room. Even I joined this one.

"Yeah, yeah." Mrs. Perez rolled her eyes. "If you want to graduate, then you have to finish your project. This year, the school board has partnered up with city council for the topic: Community Improvement!" She smiled and waited for us to cheer or something.

Someone in the back raised their hand.

"Yes?"

"So, like, what are we supposed to do?"

"I'm glad you asked. Let me pass out your project guidelines, and we'll go over it together." As soon as I received my copy, my eyes scanned the three pages. The project focused on joining a community organization whose goal was to improve our neighborhood, then write a five-page essay that highlighted our expectations, the goal, how we chose this project, etc. etc… I wiped my face in exhaustion.

"The school board wants the next generation to take part in community pride and help improve the Burrough. You can volunteer at a homeless shelter, work at city hall—"

My hand flew up. "Mrs. Perez, when is this due?"

She smiled. "On May 31$^{st}$, the last day of school."

My heart dropped. Usually, I was on top of my studies with no problem. I struggled a bit with math and science, but I passed. How the hell could I improve mi barrio and make a difference?

I met up with Nolia at lunch and slapped my brown paper bag down. It was difficult to focus on our conversation when the lunchroom was full of screaming teenagers and the foul smell of old food in the garbage. We had months to complete the project but were lost on a topic. Nolia reached into her lunch bag for leftovers. "Well, I guess it could be worse. At least this project has real purpose instead of just researching some random topic."

I ignored my leftover paella and grabbed the chocolate pudding cup. "Mhm."

Nolia flipped her braids over her shoulder. "What's up?"

"Honestly, I'm a little scared."

She smiled and gripped my hand. "Don't worry, girl. We're gonna get through this together. Why don't we go to the library after school for ideas?"

I smiled and nodded, hiding my fear. Sure, I had known one day I would discover my career and purpose. I was about to graduate and then thrown into the world of college life. And with my fibromyalgia, could I keep up? Did I need disability help?

*Pfft, Mami would love that.*

The lunch bell rang forty-five minutes later, and we made plans to meet at the entrance. During my other classes, I paid attention to the teacher, but I scribbled ideas down in my notebook, still not pleased with the results. When the school day was over, I joined Nolia outside, and we rode a bus to the library. She usually encouraged me to walk since it helped with fibro flares, but I was mentally exhausted. Throughout my classes, I had tried to think of *something* I could do with my physical limitations.

*Maybe working at a pet shelter wouldn't be so bad.*

I stored the idea away and listened to Nolia. Since she's an artist, she decided to use her talent and help children. "You know, help them get out of *el barrio* with art."

"I like that! It's beautiful."

We stepped off the bus, and Nolia held the door open to the library. This is the place to escape poverty, ignorance, and violence. I closed my eyes and inhaled, intoxicated by the scent of worn-out novels and information. Plus, the silence was divine! It was a rare treat to have quiet time between the noise of school and home. With our minds ready, we headed to the closed-off research rooms. Nolia pulled out her laptop while I perused the library for an idea.

I picked some novels off the shelves and distracted myself with young adult bestsellers, but none of the other library sections inspired me. An hour later, I headed back to Nolia. She had already sent out three application letters to community service projects that helped at-risk youth with art.

She pulled her earbuds out. "Find anything?"

I shrugged and held up some young adult novels with a sheepish smile, then glanced at the floor.

"Nichi, you're gonna find something. Don't stress."

I bit my lower lip. "I'm only stressing because I have physical limitations."

"Come on, let's take a walk and see if it clears your head. It's almost dinnertime, anyway."

I checked out the novels at the front desk, and we stepped into the frigid air. Like yesterday, the sky was a mix of grays and purples with a hint of crimson. The city came alive at night with more honking, but police sirens replaced the concrete jungle birds' songs.

Nolia asked me a bunch of questions on project ideas, but I stopped a block away from our apartments. Between two decrepit buildings was a patch of bare land with metal debris and tons of garbage. "Nichi? You okay?"

"Why would anyone just dump shit in our neighborhood like that?"

I crossed the street without waiting for her and stared at the massive junk pile. It made me sick! People had destroyed a piece of our neighborhood with harmful, useless crap. And suddenly, my neurons sparked with images of lush gardens full of Latin ingredients. We needed more trees and green space in the artificial jungle we called home.

"Nolia, I found my project."

## CHAPTER 5: LAS CHISPAS

When Nolia and I reached our block, I waved goodbye and rushed inside my apartment. Right away, Mami gave me a stern look while Isi, Willie, and Grandma had already started eating.

Mami crossed her arms. "Where were you?"

"At the library with Nolia," I said and dumped my backpack by the hallway closet. "We were brainstorming for our senior project."

Mami's eyebrows perked up while Grandma nodded in approval over her famous arroz con pollo. "What are you supposed to do?"

"Well—"

"Stop hounding her, Mari! Let the girl eat." Grandma filled up a plate piled high with rice and two chicken legs. I poured my favorite hot sauce on and dug in. For the rest of dinner, Willie and Isi babbled about what they learned at school. I focused on my food without saying a word.

Once I helped clear the dinner plates, Mami went upstairs with Willie and Isi for bath time. "Psst!" Grandma beckoned me into the kitchen. I gave her a questioning look, and she laughed. "Sorry for calling you into the kitchen like a gato. I just didn't want Mami to hear. Tell me about your senior project! Are you excited?"

I smiled. "Well, now I am. The goal is to join an organization that helps the barrio. At first, I didn't know what to do, but I'm going to plant a community garden!"

"That's wonderful, *mija*! Where are you going to start?"

I took a dish from her withered hands and dried it before putting it in the cupboard. "Near the library, there's an abandoned lot with a bunch of crap sitting around. I can start there and see where it goes."

Grandma stopped washing the dishes, and her face crinkled with worry. "It's a lot of work, and I don't want you to hurt yourself."

My smile was tight and thin. *She doesn't think I can do it. This is why I didn't tell Mami.* "I'll make it work, Grandma. It's something I'm passionate about."

She smiled and patted my shoulder with a damp hand. "Well, you know I'm here for you, baby. Your idea is wonderful!"

"Thanks, but please don't tell Mami yet. She probably wants me to work in a hospital or lawyer's office. Something that makes you rich and miserable."

Grandma laughed and reached for a beer in the fridge. "My lips are sealed."

While Grandma and I watched TV, Isi and Willie ran down in their pajamas and jumped onto the couch. "Mami said we can watch some baking shows before dinner!"

Grandma passed me the remote and drank her beer. "Oh, really?"

"YEAH!" Isi screamed.

I winced at her deafening voice, then giggled and hugged her. She smelled like a baby, fresh and clean. "Okay, let's see what's on." I flipped through the channels, ignoring the news for obvious reasons, no more Telemundo... "HGTV?" I watched a team create landscaping for a middle-class home: perfect research for my project! But of course, Willie and Isi weren't interested. "This is boring! I want *baking!*" Willie pouted. But I ignored him and listened to the TV, feeling the sparks, *las chispas*, erupt in my brain like fireworks. "I can do this," I said to myself. Grandma smiled and watched the rest of the gardening show, so I left it on. Willie and Isi fell asleep half an hour later, so we brought them upstairs to bed.

"Okay, time to play my casino games!" Grandma whispered when she finished her beer.

"Goodnight, Grandma." I kissed her cheek and headed upstairs to change into something comfortable and continued brainstorming. The *chispas* fired within my mind, a kaleidoscope of ideas, pictures, florals, and herbs. I grabbed my laptop and created a mood board of urban gardening, planting in small spaces, and researched what grew well in the Northeast.

I wrote everything I wanted to do and sketched a small map of garden beds. My phone beeped, and Nolia's name flashed across the screen.

*Hey gurl! Love your idea of a community garden and I want to help : ) But how are we gonna get permission to clear the lot?*

I smiled and texted her back. *I know just the lady to help!*

Later in the evening, I was still awake, tossing and turning, while ideas popped off in my mind, bursting forth like fireworks. I closed my eyes and tried breathing slow and deep, but a sudden thought left me breathless.

I sat up and gasped.

Papi had loved gardening.

Even in our small back patio, Papi had set up a tomato garden and planted coriander seeds for Grandma so she could have fresh cilantro through the summer. I wiped a tear away, but my emotions erupted, and I grasped my pillow.

My garden will be named *Papi's Place*.

# CHAPTER 6: AMOR?

The next morning, I rushed down the hall and ignored everyone's dumb stares and whispers. My excitement about the project fueled me until I turned into homeroom and bumped into Mrs. Perez.

"Oof! Good morning, Nichi. You look so energetic and bright today!" She raised an eyebrow when she noticed I wasn't drinking coffee.

"Mrs. Perez, I gotta talk to you before homeroom starts." I led her by the hand toward the classroom desk, and she laughed. "I haven't seen you this refreshed in a long time. What's going on?"

I pulled up a chair and crossed my legs. "It's about senior project. I found the perfect way to help the community, but I need your help."

Her smile disappeared. "Of course, Nilsa. What do you need?"

"On my way home from the library yesterday, I found an empty lot full of garbage, and I had this vision: what if I make a community garden?"

Mrs. Perez's bubbly personality returned. "That's an awesome idea! I'm proud of you for going off the beaten path and putting effort into this, Nilsa."

"But I don't know who owns the lot or how I can get approval for this. I really wanna do this, Mrs. Perez. My papi used to have a garden—" I swallowed the rest of my thought.

"Say no more. I'll bring this up at the next faculty meeting with the City Council on the project. In the meantime, think of a backup idea."

"I will. Thank you!"

But while homeroom went on as usual, I made a list of my papi's favorite vegetables and herbs.

I was in a better mood when I met Nolia at lunchtime. She smiled and unpacked her roasted pork with Caribbean seasoning. "I assume everything went well with Mrs. Perez?"

"She's agreed to help me, but we're not in the clear yet. I hope nobody owns the lot." I ripped a huge bite into my chicken sandwich seasoned with garlic, lime, and *sazón*. My eyes rolled back into my head, and I made a note to thank Grandma later.

"I doubt it." Nolia dug her fork into the tender meat. "Who keeps their property like that? Besides, if it doesn't work out, I'm sure there's another organization out there focused on urban gardening."

"Maybe. *Dios mío!* Who is that?" I practically drooled and stared at a boy with long black hair shaved on one side. He wore a delicious leather jacket adorned with chains.

And were those Doc Martens?

I rested my head in my hands and stared at this masterpiece. Finally, a hot punk boy in *my* school! My taste in piercings, tattoos, and leather always puzzled Nolia, Mami, and Grandma. Mami had pointed out the boys in our neighborhood, and I made a disgusted face. "Why not the normal boys?" she had begged.

Nolia turned to follow my gaze, then leaned into my vision and laughed. "Nichi, that's a girl."

My cheeks burned. "No way!"

"Yes, I'm serious. She's in my homeroom, and this is her first day. I'll call them over. Jayden!"

I almost protested, but then my stomach dropped once I saw Jayden's face. Ice-blue eyes and glossed lips only added to her beauty, and her ripped jeans hugged her small curves perfectly—did I mention the Doc Martens?

My mouth suddenly felt dry, and I lost my appetite. *Seriously, that's a girl?*

Jayden smiled and waved at Nolia, then headed in our direction.

*Crap, crap, crap!* I had eaten the most garlicky chicken ever! My earlier praise of Grandma's food changed as I dug into my purse and popped a mint in my mouth. A chair scraped next to mine, and I froze.

"Hey, Nolia, right? You're in my homeroom."

"Yup! And this is my friend Nichi."

"Hi," my shaking hand reached out toward their firm one, and I hoped my palm wasn't sweaty. Underneath my hand, I felt rough calouses.

"I'm Jayden. Nice to meet you!"

I stared blankly for a minute before smiling. "Same."

Jayden's hand lingered before pulling away to ruffle her shiny black hair.

Nolia tried not to burst out laughing. "So, you said you moved from Philly?"

"Yeah!" Jayden brightened. "My dad is a professor, so we move around a lot in the Northeast based on what's available."

"What does he teach?" I asked.

"His specialty is medieval literature, but he also teaches classics and all that. I guess that's where I get my love of lit from."

"I love books," I muttered, slightly embarrassed.

To my utter shock, she laughed, which made my cheeks redden even more.

"What's your next class?"

I realized after a pause that Jayden was talking to me. "Oh! Um, American literature."

"Same! I'll meet you there. Save me a seat." Jayden waved and floated to another group so effortlessly. I watched her walk away until Nolia smacked my arm and smirked.

"What?" I mumbled.

"Girl, you got it bad."

"*Ay, Callate*. I'm just socially nervous."

"Is that what they call it?"

I shot her a look, and we ate in silence. But once the bell rang, and we filed out of the cafeteria, Jayden's devilish smile invaded my mind.

But *me*? And a girl?

*I must have fibro brain fog again.*

Once I walked into the classroom, Jayden rested her foot on the seat next to her but moved it once they saw me. Usually I sat in the front, but I didn't want to be rude.

*No,* I tell myself. *It's not because Jayden is hot.*

I drummed my fingers on my textbook before turning in my seat. "So, are you all caught up with our latest readings? If not, I can help you."

She smirked. "I think I'll be okay, thanks."

"Oh." I turned back toward the front, wishing I hadn't said anything.

But before class started, she tapped my shoulder. "Here." She scribbled on a piece of paper and handed it to me.

I unraveled it and read their phone number with a winky face.

I didn't spend time with my family after dinner. There was a lot in my head that needed sorting, like one of Mami's crochet yarn balls. I leaned on my closed bedroom door and sweat trickled down my scalp.

*Since when do I like girls? Sure, girls are pretty, but so are boys.*

I grabbed my phone and dialed Nolia's number. "*Ay*, Nich. You still trippin' over Jayden, right?"

I waited a moment, then covered my face with a pillow.

"I hear you breathing." Nolia laughed.

"Okay, okay! Jayden is hot, and I like her! But I just—what if Mami finds out?"

Nolia sighed, and I knew she understood what I meant. In Spanish households, our customs are old-fashioned. Women cook, clean, and pop out babies, while men work and fix the house. These roles are rarely altered.

"Nichi, we live in the twenty-first century! People create themselves and live authentic truths. Besides, if your mama has a problem with you dating a girl, then I'll tell her to have a seat."

I stifled my laugh and imagined Mami's reaction.

"Listen, you don't have to figure everything out about yourself right away. I got you, love."

"Thanks Nolia."

"Now, I gotta get back to my homework, but we'll talk more in the morning. Love you!" She hung up, and I stared at my phone screen with the crumpled paper in my hand. I closed my eyes and inhaled while entering the number in my phone.

*Hey it's Nichi : ) What's up?*

A few moments passed by before my phone buzzed.

*Nothin much! How was your day?:)*

*Pretty good! Nervous about my senior project, but I'm going to start a new novel tonight. We need to catch up and talk books!*

*Come see me at lunch tomorrow. It was awesome meeting you : )*

# CHAPTER 7: PASTELITOS

The next month was hell as I waited for Mrs. Perez. Every day when I stepped into homeroom, I glanced hopefully in her direction but was told "not yet," or "still waiting for City Council." I sighed in frustration and considered other ideas. Maybe the animal shelter? After school homework tutoring? Hell, I even added clerical stuff, even though it wasn't my passion. The stress of waiting killed my body, and my bones ached with a flu-like pain. But I stuck to my original idea until Mrs. Perez greeted me with an excited smile.

"Tell me everything!"

"The good news is, the city doesn't have any record of private ownership, and they want it cleaned up ASAP. Here's a letter that grants you access to the lot for the project." She passed me the page.

"You said good news, so I expect something else is attached to this?"

She sighed. "The bad news is they expect you to clean it up by this weekend or else they'll put the lot up for sale."

"What? Why would they do that? I'm trying to help the community!"

Mrs. Perez shrugged and shook her head. "This is a serious undertaking, Nilsa, and they want to see your commitment. I need pictures by Monday morning on your progress."

I smiled and nodded, but underneath my façade, my stomach dropped. There was some serious garbage on the lot! How could I move it all by myself? I know Nolia would help, maybe Jayden, but we needed a team.

"Oh, here's a list of resources in the community willing to offer their services." She leafed through a file and handed me a list of shops and small companies offering secondhand equipment or advice. On the list was the shop my Tío Miguel worked at, my estranged uncle who Mami liked to call *basura* or garbage. I've always kept in touch with him thanks to Grandma, and I was due for a visit.

In between classes, I glared at the sickly red and hot pink Valentine's Day decorations and puckered my lips like I had tasted a bad guava. The candy-filled, sappy holiday was this weekend, and the school was hosting a dance on Friday night. Of course, I wasn't going and *of course* I wasn't asking a certain someone with beautiful blue eyes and feathery black hair heading in my direction.

I forced myself to make eye contact with Jayden, and she waved, then shuffled through the crowd toward me. For the last few weeks, Jayden and I had exchanged casual texts and talked at lunch. She loved the same bands and pop music as me, but we shared our love of literature, especially classics like Poe, Chopin, Yeats, and others we had learned about in class. I thought back to one of our first conversations and bit my cheek to stop smirking.

"I just feel that Kate Chopin's work is—"

"Underrated?" I grinned.

"Yes!"

Nolia had always sat on the other side of the table and watched with unabashed curiosity as we talked and exchanged "googly eyes" as she had pointed out.

Now, Jayden walked toward me, and I leaned on the lockers in a sad attempt to look casual. "Hey, Nich!" She opened her free arm to give me a hug. I closed my eyes for a moment and inhaled her sweet, fruity perfume.

"Hi!" We pulled away and avoided each other's eyes for a moment. I gestured to the Valentine's Day décor. "Can you believe this crap?"

Jayden laughed and ruffled her hair. "Yeah, to each his own, right? How is your senior project coming along? Did you get permission yet?"

I pulled out the paper like a trophy. "Yeah, everything's good."

"That's awesome! Congrats!"

"Well, there's a catch. I have to clean up the entire lot this weekend *and* take pictures. Mrs. Perez said the City Council wants proof that I'm committed. I don't know what I'm gonna do! I don't have the money to hire help, and I can't do it by myself."

Jayden put a hand on my shoulder and forced me to look up. "Who said you're doing it by yourself? You know me and Nolia are here. As for more people…" She tapped her foot until her icy eyes lit up.

"Have you considered a bake sale? You know, outside the gym for the Valentine's Day dance? Everyone wants chocolate and delicious sweets, especially that night! I can also create a funding page. I'm working at a bakery for my senior project. We make gourmet treats on the weekend and donate them to churches and foodbanks."

I smiled at her willingness to help. Jayden chose culinary arts, specifically baking, for her senior project. She had found an organization that hosted monthly community bake sales and donated the profits to the local food bank. "Really? You would do that for me?"

"Of course! Why do you ask?"

I blushed and shrugged.

The bell rang overhead, and the hallway cleared. "Let's meet up at lunch and go over this more! See you!" Jayden waved and headed down the hall at a light jog.

I slapped my hand over my face.

If the school allowed the bake sale, Grandma was going to kill me for the last-minute chaos.

At lunchtime, the three of us munched in silence before moving onto the bake sale idea. We each wrote a list of our favorites and combined them for a streamlined menu.

Nolia tapped her pencil on her chin. "I have *flan* and *tres leches*. I bet those will be popular, and they're easy to make."

I nodded. "I have those on my list too, and maybe we could make empanadas filled with guava and cheese. Or even *brazo gitano*!"

"What's that?" Jayden asked while scribbling more ideas.

"It's basically a roulade cake, but it's filled with guava jam and cream cheese." I sighed in happiness while remembering our trips to Puerto Rico. It was always the first treat to buy on our list.

"Sounds good!" Jayden grinned. "I don't have anything super exotic like you guys; just chocolate hazelnut cupcakes and double chocolate chip cookies."

I tore another sheet of paper from my notebook. "We can't do everything, or else Grandma will have a fit. Let's see…"

"I can make the cupcakes and cookies myself," Jayden said.

I scribbled the treats under her name.

"So instead of flan, let's go with the *tres leches* and empanadas. They'll be easier to make in batches."

We agreed on our ideas, but then my heart sank. "We forgot to ask for permission! I can't believe I—"

"Nich, everything is fine." Jayden rested her hand on my shoulder. "I already asked the principal before talking to you in the hall, just in case. He's fine with the idea since it's for the senior project. We just have to put any allergen warnings in front of the desserts."

I was so relieved I could've kissed Jayden. "Thank you, thank you! This is gonna be so much fun!"

After lunch, we agreed to text each other later. Jayden lingered outside the cafeteria doors and ruffled her hair. "Wanna walk to class together?"

I nodded, trying to keep my excitement to a minimum. But even when we sat down next to each other in English class, I barely focused on the teacher's lecture and daydreamed about guava, chocolate, and Jayden's perfume.

"Grandma! I'm home! I gotta talk to you about something *super* important, but don't be mad." I set my backpack down by the door and hung my coat up in the closet. Pots and pans banged around as she prepared dinner. My stomach growled at the spicy scent of garlic, cilantro, and chorizo.

"Come in the kitchen, *mija*. Mami is still at work, so I want to finish dinner before she gets home." It was a miracle how Grandma kept every burner and inch of the countertop full of fried chicken, *arroz con candules*, and salad. "I hope we can eat soon, Grandma. This looks amazing."

She chuckled and patted her fluffy white hair. "*Gracias, mija.* Now, what did you want to talk about?"

I bit the corner of my cheek and twisted my hands. "Well, you know how I'm working on my senior project for the community."

"Mhm." She stirred the rice.

"Mrs. Perez said the City Council wants me to clean up the lot this weekend to show initiative. But I know that's going to cost money, so my friend suggested we have a bake sale."

She stopped and turned around, a puzzled expression creasing her features. "Why don't you just ask Tío Miguel for help? I'm sure he would do it for free."

"Oh! I hadn't thought of that, but I'll still need money to buy plants and soil and—"

"Okay, so when is this bake sale?"

"Friday night."

"*¡Coño!*" She covered her mouth. "Okay, but you're helping me, Nichi. And make sure to pick up the ingredients I write on the list tomorrow so we can be ready Thursday night."

"Of course! Nolia and my friend Jayden even offered to come by and help."

"Good. We'll need all the help we can get. Let's just keep the kitchen clean. You know how Mami gets with mess and stuff everywhere."

"Thank you, Grandma! You're the best."

She chuckled and gave me a kiss. "*Mi amor*, I would do anything for you."

After dinner, I went into my closet to talk to Gaia. It had been a while since I connected with the Goddess, and now more than ever, I needed Her help. I sat cross-legged in front of my small altar and spread some incense across the surface. I envisioned the flames of my blue and white candles, then closed my eyes.

"Good evening, Goddess. I know it's been some time since we last spoke, and I apologize for not acknowledging you. Things have been getting crazy— in a good way. Thank you for blessing me with a supportive family and friends, and for giving me purpose again. Thank you for my health and for potentially finding love." I smiled as I thought about Jayden. "As I continue this project, I ask for your blessing. It's going to be tough, but I can do it. I know I can. Thank you, Gaia. Blessed Be." I made the sign of the pentagram and imagined the candles slowly dimming.

"Oh, and say hi to Papi. I hope he's proud of me."

# CHAPTER 8: AZUCAR!

After school, I rushed to every store and bodega in the neighborhood to find Grandma's ingredients. Thankfully, the bodegas had most of the stuff she needed, like guava paste for the empanadas. My mouth watered as I thought about biting into a crispy pastry with a burst of tropical filling and cream cheese.

On Thursday afternoon, Jayden and Nolia walked home with me, although I noticed Nolia smirked and tried to give us some room to talk. I urged her to keep up, but she waved me off.

The air was frigid, and I savored every moment. In a few months, the barrio would be a stifling oven of concrete, meaning I was going to flare more. For now, I relished every kiss of frost on my skin. Jayden's gorgeous blue eyes took in mi barrio with a mixture of curiosity and wonder. "I love the cold weather. It's so comfortable and makes you alert and feel alive, you know?"

I nodded. "The best holidays happen in the fall and winter months, plus the summers here are horrible. No pools, no beaches, and crappy air conditioning."

We continued down the block, Nolia and I waving to our Latin neighbors and introducing Jayden. But all the pleasantries escaped us once I unlocked my apartment door and Grandma stood like a drill sergeant in the kitchen. "You're late! I told you three, and it's three fifteen. Where have you been? Oh, hi Nolia! How are you, baby?"

"Abuelita!" Nolia rushed into the kitchen to hug Grandma and kissed her cheek. Nolia never met her grandmother before she passed away, so she always had a special relationship with mine.

"Grandma! I was just walking home! Jeez. And this is Jayden, my new friend from school."

Grandma smiled and opened her arms. "Welcome to our home, Jayden." Grandma smothered her in a big hug, and Jayden laughed. "Thank you so much! I already finished the cookies and cupcakes last night, so I wanted to help."

"I'm glad Nichi has such amazing friends like you two. Okay girls, let's get started." She handed us rag-tag aprons. Suddenly, Isi and Willie rushed into the apartment with Mami. She kicked off her heels and hung my siblings' jackets up in the closet. I hugged both tightly while Nolia kissed the little ones, but they were shy around Jayden and hid behind my legs. I giggled and pushed them forward.

"So, are these the two troublemakers of the house? You must be princess Isi and Master Willie!" Jayden bowed like a medieval noble, and the kids laughed. During the weeks we exchanged texts, I told Jayden how much my siblings meant to me. Mami ushered them into the living room and put their favorite cartoon on, then came back into the kitchen.

"Hola Nolia! How's your mami?" She kissed my best friend and turned toward Jayden. I braced for impact, but Mami surprised me. "Hi there! Are you Jayden? Nichi mentioned you're the new girl at school."

Jayden smiled, and I blushed. Nolia noticed and elbowed my ribs playfully. "It's nice to meet you! Nichi and Nolia have been the nicest people to me so far." She extended her hand out, but Mami pulled her into a gentle hug.

Nolia and I stared at each other with widened eyes. *Who is this woman?! She never greets new people like this!*

"Okay, ladies. I'll get out of your way as soon as I grab a snack for the kids."

On the other counter, Grandma prepared the buttery pastry for the empanadas and kneaded it gently until everything came together. "Okay, everyone grab a small piece like this, then gently flatten it out with your hands until it's a six-inch circle. Got it?"

"Yes, ma'am!" we said in unison. Soon, we became an empanada factory and formed the dough into smooth circles. Grandma instructed Jayden how to cut up the guava and cream cheese, then place enough for a substantial filling. "You must be careful. If you overfill them, they explode in the fryer!" Grandma chuckled and told us how she learned the hard way when she had first made them as a young woman in Puerto Rico. It took us a few hours, but by six o'clock, we had fried 50 empanadas! Grandma wiped her brow as she stood over the stove, laboring over each pastry until it turned into golden goodness. We each split the first one, and my eyes rolled back. Even Jayden loved the flavor after trying guava for the first time.

"Okay, no more tasting!" Grandma playfully swatted our hands and stored the finished empanadas in the fridge. When we ran out of storage space, Nolia offered to take some home and rushed across the street.

In the meantime, we began the *tres leches* cake batter and whisked the dry ingredients while Grandma whipped the egg whites to stiff peaks. Nolia came back and prepared the soaking mixture. Multiple batches went into the oven while Jayden and I assembled each layer with Grandma's careful instructions. By the time we had finished, it was midnight. I could tell Grandma was tired as she wiped her brow again and drank a <u>*malta*</u> at the kitchen table.

"We'll clean up, Abuelita," Nolia said.

"*Gracias, mija.* I'm going to watch my shows since I have the living room to myself."

"Thanks again, Grandma!"

"*Te quiero, mija.* Good luck." She kissed my forehead and shuffled away.

Even though we were exhausted and desperate to try our creations, it was worth the effort. Grandma poured her love into every ounce of filling, pastry, and cake. I scrubbed a pan and started crying. Sure, I've cried in front of Nolia plenty of times, but I was so embarrassed to weep in front of Jayden.

"Nich? What's wrong?" Nolia grabbed my shoulders and Jayden stopped mid-rinse.

"I feel so grateful for having you both in my life. Seriously, I wouldn't have pulled this off with just Grandma and me. And you're helping me clean the lot on Saturday—"

Jayden and Nolia wrapped their arms around me, and just like the *tres leches* cake, I soaked up their beautiful love.

Friday afternoon, I couldn't contain my excitement as Nolia, Jayden, and I met up to grab the pastries. They believed I would raise enough money to cover the gardening costs, but I still had doubts. After all, I was the school outcast. I bit my lip and tried not to cry as I thought about our long night laboring over sweets that would go to waste, especially since I couldn't eat any of it because of the gluten.

Since we had so many pastries, Mami drove us to school. Usually, our family doesn't use the car. We hadn't serviced it since Papi was alive, another harsh reminder of his absence. But we couldn't possibly carry all of this ourselves on the bus.

"Good luck tonight!" Mami called out the window as we struggled with the mounds of empanadas, *tres leches* cake, cupcakes, and cookies. The heavenly aromas made my stomach growl. Despite Jayden and Nolia's protests, I hadn't eaten lunch since I was so anxious. There were a few faculty and students still hovering around the hallways before the dance, including Mrs. Perez. She smiled as she passed by. "Those look fantastic! I'll come by and take one of each!"

"Thank you!" We called back in unison.

The cafeteria workers had set up a table for us. We placed the pastries on colorful pink paper plates and had a list of prices and potential allergens. Jayden listed the empanadas and *tres leches* cake for three dollars and fifty cents, but the cookies and cupcakes were four dollars a serving!

"Aren't the prices too high for a school bake sale?" Nolia said.

Jayden smiled and continued setting up the treats. "Nah, don't worry. When people want chocolate, they'll pay anything."

I trusted her and shrugged my shoulders while Nolia set up the debit card payment option on her phone. Once the dance began and students rolled in, they immediately stopped in front of our bake sale. Some idiots shot questioning glares between me and the pastries, but when they noticed Jayden and Nolia, empanadas flew off the table.

Everything looked great, and our cash box was filling up when Talia sauntered to the table.

"Aww how cute! The girl scouts are here!" Talia grinned like a vicious cat about to kill a mouse. The girls beside her laughed.

I sighed and rolled my eyes. "Just buy something or get lost! I'm trying to work on senior project, unlike you."

Talia's red nail skimmed the plate of a *tres leches* slice, and it plopped to the floor. I gasped.

"What's wrong with you?" Nolia shook her head and grabbed napkins to clean up the mess.

But Jayden grabbed Talia by her faux fur jacket collar. "If you don't pay for that, you're going to fucking regret it," she said through gritted teeth.

Talia rolled her eyes and shrugged out of Jayden's grasp. But behind that ghetto princess façade, her confidence wavered. She dropped a five-dollar bill on the table and trudged inside the gym, where loud house music shook the floors.

"Jayden!" I squealed and threw my arms around her.

She chuckled in my ear and held me for a moment. "Don't let them talk to you like that. A pretty girl like you doesn't deserve it."

Nolia grinned, and I could tell she ate this up like Grandma's desserts. For the rest of the night, we made slow but steady progress with our pastry sales, and a few of my teachers, including Mrs. Perez, kept their promise to support us. Her eyes rolled back when she tasted Grandma's empanada. "Takes me back to my grandma's pastries!"

Half an hour before the dance was over, we sold out of everything. Nolia rushed to check the sales on her phone while Jayden counted the cash drawer. "Oh my God, Nichi! We made five hundred dollars."

I almost choked on my water, and Jayden slapped my back. "Holy crap!" I peeked over Nolia's shoulder to check the calculator, then pulled them into a hug. "I can't thank you both enough for your help. Do you want some money to cover—"

"Girl, stop tripping!" Nolia pushed my shoulder, and Jayden held her hand out. "No way! We did this for you. And we'll help you tomorrow, too!"

I peeked into the gym and noticed couples dancing to the final slow songs of the night.

Nolia took the hint and texted her mom for a ride home. "You guys have fun!"

I desperately wanted her to come back. Now Jayden and I stood by the table in awkward silence. I blushed when she flipped her hair.

"Nich, I don't know if I'm reading this wrong, but do you wanna dance?"

I nodded, and she grabbed my hand. With my other one, I pulled my black curls free from my ponytail. Everyone was dressed up while we were in jeans and t-shirts, but I didn't care. Jayden's calloused hand gripped mine and wrapped the other around my waist. I felt like I was floating off the floor, like we were the only ones in the gym, swaying under the dimmed lights. I leaned my forehead on hers, and her fingers tangled in my curls. A few people pointed in our direction, but it didn't matter.

Because Jayden leaned in and kissed me. I met her lips willingly, savoring her scent, the feeling of her body close to mine. The lights abruptly turned on, and everyone filed out, yet we still held each other. I blushed and smiled, gently pulling away.

Jayden reached for my hand. "Can I walk you home?"

"Of course."

We took our time sauntering down the street, unspoken thoughts as we replayed the kiss in our minds.

We took some detours to avoid heading home. Jayden said her dad wouldn't care, but she didn't know the wrath of a Puerto Rican mom. I dismissed my guilt and enjoyed the moment. It had been so long since I felt a connection with anyone. The previous jerk I dated broke up with me a week after Papi died.

"So."

"So?" I smiled and leaned into her.

"Are you okay dating a girl? I mean, not that we're dating, but maybe we are—"

"I don't mind, but you're the first girl I've kissed."

Jayden nervously chuckled. "What did you think?"

I stopped in front of her and kissed her lips. "I kinda like it." Jayden smirked under my lips, and we continued down the dark streets, void of stars but full of barrio life; car horns, taxis, and old men screaming about their domino games. Women gossiped with one another about their family members, and kids our age loitered on stoops while smoking weed.

We passed the empty lot and stopped, taking in our big chore.

"I'm so glad my dad moved us here. We struggle sometimes with the bills and all but— you're going to do great things here, Nichi."

I sighed. "Jayden, do you know why I asked you and Nolia to help me?"

She shrugged. "Well, look at this place."

"No, it's not just that. I have an autoimmune disease called fibromyalgia. It causes constant exhaustion and excruciating pain. I always feel like this—all because—"

"Hey, don't cry." She wiped my cheek, and my eyes widened. I hadn't felt the tears cascading down my face. I realized I hadn't told her about Papi yet. It was still too raw, too traumatic to discuss between flirty texts. "I'm not bothered at all. It's okay to ask for help, whether you're sick or healthy. I like you because you're pretty, gentle, and funny. We have the same interests and ambitions to get out of high school and make a difference. None of the other things matter or make me think less of you."

I hugged Jayden and buried my face in her neck. She held me for a moment and kissed my cheek.

"Let's get you home. And remember, you can tell me what happened whenever you're ready."

We walked on in silence, a new somber feeling stretching between our bliss. At my apartment door, Jayden leaned in for a kiss when Mami snapped the door open, and I pulled away.

"Nilsa! Where the hell were you? You said the dance ended at nine and it's eleven thirty!"

Jayden stepped in front of me. "I apologize, Mrs. Rivera. It was my fault. I asked Nilsa for a tour of the neighborhood, and we stopped at the lot to talk about plans for tomorrow. Anyways, goodnight!"

I trudged into the house and gave Mami the stink eye behind her back.

---

After I grabbed a plate of leftovers, I went into the bathroom to take my makeup off. Downstairs, Mami's cell phone rang, and I recognized the ringtone: Tia Flora. I heard them talk in murmured Spanish, and then Mami's voice raised. She's usually good at keeping her voice down for the neighbors and the kids upstairs, but she went on a rampage.

"*¡Oye, Mari! Cálmate!*" Grandma hissed, urging Mami to be quiet.

"No!" And then she rushed on in rapid Spanish. I heard Tío Miguel's name, followed by a screaming match with Grandma. I rolled my eyes and headed into my room, too exhausted by the day's events. Instead, I grabbed my phone and texted the infamous Tío Miguel, asking if I could meet him the next morning at the hardware store.

## CHAPTER 9: TIAS Y TIOS

In Puerto Rican culture, family means everything, and the cost is profound if someone breaks this golden rule.

Tío Miguel left Puerto Rico when he was sixteen. He needed space.

Tía Flora stuck by Mami and Grandma's side. She learned the charms of womanhood.

Tío Miguel joined gangs, sold drugs, and went to jail. He almost died from a knife wound.

Tía Flora waited until she was "of age" to leave the house when a rich man offered her a better life in California.

Tío Miguel repented for his sins and apologized to Grandma and his sisters. Only one sister forgave him, and it was Tía Flora.

But Mami was always the glue trying to hold everyone together, always in the middle of big fights and family heartaches. Mami was neither a slum dog like Tío nor a socialite like Tía. Instead, she was just Mami, the woman with three kids and a dead husband.

And she never felt good enough.

## CHAPTER 10: MIGUEL'S PROMISE

The next morning, my body begged me to stay in bed after tossing and turning all night, especially since Mami and Grandma had argued for a while. But once my alarm on my phone beeped at seven AM, I reminded myself of the commitment I made to Papi's memory. I rubbed the sleepiness out of my eyes, stretched, then texted Jayden and Nolia that I was going to be late this morning. *Getting more backup!* I explained. They sent a thumbs up emoji, and then I dressed in yoga pants and a t-shirt.

Although it was still cold outside, I knew I would sweat from all the hard work, so I wanted to be comfortable. I pinned my hair up in a clip and fluffed my black curls, then studied myself in the mirror. Huh. I had a strange radiant glow in my eyes, then blushed when I remembered Jayden's lips. Even though we were doing yard work, I wanted to make sure I looked the best. It felt weird to put effort into my appearance.

When I headed downstairs, Isi and Willie were watching their favorite cartoons while Grandma prepared eggs and toast. Judging by her stern expression and tight lips, she was still pissed about last night's fight.

"Good morning!" I kissed my brother and sister, who latched onto my neck playfully as I stumbled into the kitchen. "I have to talk to Grandma for a minute," I told them between giggles, "but then we can eat together."

They rushed out of the room and hopped back onto the couch. I was so jealous of their morning energy.

I kissed Grandma's cheek, and she stopped cooking eggs to hug me. "Grandma, what happened last night? I feel like every time Tia Flora calls—"

"No, Nichi." She pulled away and held my shoulders. "This wasn't about Tia Flora. Your mami refuses to forgive Tío Miguel for his past mistakes. She still sees him as a criminal instead of family, and it hurts my heart." She sighed and shook her head. "Are you still keeping in touch with him?"

"Of course. He's always been good to me. I don't care what happened in the past. In fact, I'm heading to the hardware store today. Wanna come?"

"Good, good. And I can't. I have to watch the little ones and promised to take them to the park. But say hello and give my love."

I scarfed down my eggs before my brother and sister sat down, then headed out the door to meet up with Mami's number one enemy: her brother.

The hardware store was a few blocks away, and I turned down winding streets in *mi barrio*. When I pushed the squeaky door open and heard the bell overhead, strange smells assaulted my memory. There was fresh sawdust, motor oil, and the clank of tools. I instantly thought of Papi's old garage and bit my lip as my eyes watered. *Don't do this. Not today.* I needed to be strong and focused on new beginnings. A memory suddenly flooded me with emotion, broken images that led up to one moment. I was a little girl, and Papi had taken me to work.

I had watched in fascination as his hands rebuilt cars and helped fix our neighbor's broken hedge trimmers or tinker with replacement parts.

"Papi, I wanna be like you some day!"

He chuckled and kissed my head. "Thanks, baby. How about you come with me to fix Mrs. Garcia's stove?"

I wiped a tear away and breathed in before searching the aisles for my tio. I found him stocking tools and waited for him to finish. He was a towering man with a bald scalp, and tattoos were scattered down his neck in random spots like wall graffiti. Some of them snaked up his skull. He had gained some weight since the last time I saw him, but I still found reflections of Mami and Grandma in his features.

"Can I help you—Hey, Nich! Come here!" He lifted me up in a bear hug and kissed my cheek.

I hugged him back and laughed. "How are you, Tío?"

He shrugged and smiled. "Same old, same old. Working here, community service there. I got your text last night. You know, I was so happy to hear from you. How's your mami?"

It was my turn to shrug, but instead of smiling, I rolled my eyes. "You know the deal. Still judgmental, everyone's wrong, same old."

He nodded and put a tool away.

"So, Tío, I'm working on a senior community service project. I have an abandoned lot I want to turn into a community garden. There's some heavy stuff there, and tons of garbage! Do you think you can help? I can pay you—"

"What? Nichi, don't talk like that. We're family. Of course, I'll help you!" Tío studied his cracked watch. "I get off at two, but I'll text a few of my buddies to help out."

I jumped up and hugged him. "Thank you, Tio!" I smacked kiss after kiss on his cheek.

He patted my back. "No worries, *mija*. You said you're doing this for the community? Man, I'm so proud of you. After all my past mistakes, I really want to help make this neighborhood a better place and inspire kids your age. I never want someone to experience what I did in jail."

I crossed my arms. "Will you ever tell me about it?"

"Hah! Nichi, your brain is too beautiful for the violence of my past. Don't worry about it."

I walked out of the store with newfound hope and focused on the word "proud." It was nice to hear it from another family member other than Grandma.

# CHAPTER 11: THE CLEANUP

When I arrived at the lot, Jayden and Nolia were already cleaning up and tossed the smaller debris at the grass line's edge.

"Good news! My Tío Miguel is coming this afternoon with some of his guys. They'll help us move the bigger stuff."

"That's awesome!" Jayden said.

Nolia gave the thumbs up sign while hauling a load of garbage into a disposable bag. She already had a rip in her washed-out jeans, and her tank top had a mystery stain on it. Jayden passed me a pair of work gloves and winked at me. She wore a black T-shirt and baggy shorts. "You look cute today," she whispered.

"Who me? In these yoga pants?" I smiled, fishing for more compliments.

"All of you, Nich." She kissed my forehead before moving on to help Nolia.

I shoved my gloves on and took a deep breath. This was it; the first step to making this place look amazing. I trudged over mountains of stuff and scrap metal to continue Nolia and Jayden's work. But as we dragged more debris toward the curb, I couldn't believe the foul stench leaching out of the ground. I held my breath while I moved another bag, and Nolia gagged.

"What in the hell?" The smell permeated my mouth and nose.

Jayden waved the air in front of her. "It's probably all the crap rotting here. Who knows what else we'll uncover?"

A few hours later, we sat on the curb, out of breath and sweaty. We had run out of room to move the garbage elsewhere and waited for Tío. Nolia passed around ice-cold water bottles she had brought, but I was so drenched in sweat that I just wanted to pour it over my head. So far, I didn't have any deep aches in my joints, but *oh*, I knew it was coming after seeing how much more work we had to do.

An enormous dump truck turned the corner and parked in front of our lot. Tío stepped out with a grin. "What do you think? This should be good, right?"

"Tío! Thank God you're here. We can't keep moving the stuff around. There's no room!"

A few more cars rolled up, and Tío's friends stepped out with industrial-sized garbage bags. I recognized a couple of them since they worked alongside

Tío at the hardware store. They greeted us with simple waves and went to work. We stood up, stretched, and dove back into the pile.

Tío and his friends hoisted an old stove away and threw it in the truck with a sickening metal screech. We worked like a factory line; Nolia, Jayden, and I packed up garbage bags while Tío and his friends tossed them into the truck. A few bags ripped open and revealed their foul-smelling contents. I shook my head, sickened that people had thrown away their weekly garbage here with no pride in our barrio.

Honestly, I felt like total shit by the end of the day. I stunk like filth rotting under the sun, and my joints were screaming in pain. I turned to Nolia and Jayden, who were also sweaty but didn't seem bothered by the physical labor. At first, I felt a sting of jealousy and resentment. *Why does my body always betray me?* But then I surveyed the lot and how it turned into a blank canvas because of my loved ones. I pictured tomatoes there, and a row of jalapenos there. The *chispa* took over again, lighting a proud fire in my belly. I finally felt a purpose after a year of sorrow, but instead of moping, I smiled through the pain.

"Hey, Nichi. Come here, you need to see this."

My spark wavered when I headed over to Tío. He bent down on one knee and ran the gritty soil through his stained glove. "We can't plant anything in the ground. It's got a ton of motor oil and other contaminants. The plants will absorb it, and it could make people sick."

"What are we going to do? We put so much effort into this!"

"Chill, *mija*," he chuckled. "We'll just build raised beds. I'll grab some reclaimed composite decking and untreated wood from the recycling center, and then we'll line it a thick layer of paving stones and mulch, so the chemicals won't seep into the new dirt."

"I can give you some money if you—"

"Girl, stop with that talk. You sound just like your mami!" He sighed. "I'm sorry. *Nobody* sounds like your mami. But please, let me help you. I want to do this for my community and my oldest niece, okay?"

I nodded and smiled, then gripped him in a sweaty hug. Just as we tossed more bags into the dump truck, we heard a soft mewling sound from the lot's corner. My heart fluttered with an instinct to protect kicking in. The sound reminded me of Isi or Willie when they scraped their knees. I turned and found a fuzzy, orange animal hiding behind the last clutter.

"Nich, be careful!" Nolia whispered.

Jayden crouched next to me and waited. "I think it's a cat."

"Come on, baby." I called in my sweetest voice. "We won't hurt you. Pssst, pssst, pssst, here kitty, kitty!"

An orange tabby stuck its head around a junk pile, then ducked back around it. I chuckled at its naïve survival skills. "Come on, baby! Let me see your pretty kitty face."

The cat slipped around the corner again, peering at all of us, and crawled to me with its tail between its legs. A piece of his ear was gone, and his fur was matted. But I held my hand out and waited while he sniffed, then he nuzzled my arm. It was a plea for help that caused my eyes to tear. "Do you wanna come home with me, sweetie? You can have a nice warm bed and plenty of food."

As if he understood, the cat nuzzled harder and purred, then had the courage to say hello to everyone with a loud meow.

Tío chuckled while scratching the cat, and he arched his back. "So, what's his name?"

I pursed my lips and thought for a moment. "I'll call him... Cheese!"

"*Cheese?*" Nolia burst out laughing. "Well, he looks like a good slice of cheddar."

"Sir Cheese it is!" Jayden declared.

We decided to finish cleaning up the rest of the junk next week, and Tío drove us and Cheese back to the apartment. Nolia and Jayden wished me luck with the kitty, then headed home to rest and shower.

I turned the key in the apartment lock, and my heart thudded. I could tell Cheese was nervous in my arms, so I held him for a moment and scratched his head. "Don't worry, buddy. Welcome to your new home."

---

"*Ay mija! Qué es? Oh, pobrecito!*" rushed out of Grandma's mouth when I brought Cheese inside.

"He's a stray living in the junk at the empty lot. I couldn't leave him there!"

"You have such a good heart, *mija.*" She stepped closer to Cheese and held out her hand. He sniffed eagerly, then licked her hand with gusto. Grandma let out a bellowing laugh, and Cheese tried to run. "I just finished cooking, so he must have good taste! I'll boil some chicken and rice. Go upstairs and get him cleaned up before your mami comes home!"

Willie and Isi peaked out the door and almost screamed in delight. "No! Kitty is very scared and needs a bath. You need to be quiet for a while until he gets comfortable, okay?"

They nodded and watched from across the hall while I drew Cheese a warm bath. You know the usual joke about cats hating water? Sure, he was nervous, but once I dipped his toes in and scrubbed away the dirt and drowned those fleas, his nervous cries for help turned into relaxed purrs. After a quick towel dry and brushing, he looked like a new boy. In fact, he seemed to strut around the apartment in pride, checking out different rooms and even smelled Willie's and Isi's hands. Isi sneezed, and I was concerned her seasonal allergies would become worse, but I saw adoration in her eyes when she stroked Cheese's back.

"Here kitty, kitty!" Grandma called from downstairs. Cheese's ears perked up, and he rushed into the kitchen. Before I made it down to the last step, he was gobbling up the chicken and rice bits, then slurped up an entire bowl of water.

"Good boy!" Grandma patted his butt while Cheese sauntered back up the stairs for a full-belly nap.

"What's his name?"

I giggled and covered my mouth. "Cheese."

"*Cheese?* Why?"

"I mean, look at his beautiful fur! It's like a beautiful slice of cheddar."

Grandma rolled her eyes and laughed.

Our apartment door opened and Mami walked in, kicked off her heels as usual, and sighed. "*Hola.*"

"Hi," Grandma and I said in unison.

She raised an eyebrow and stopped taking off her coat. "Why do you have weird looks on your faces? And why are there bowls on the floor?" And then her eyes widened.

"What did you *do,* Nichi?"

"Okay, before you explode, a stray cat needed my help while we cleaned up the lot. Please, just give him a chance, Mami!"

"Do we have food, a litter box? No!"

I sighed and dragged her up the stairs into my room. I creaked the door open to show her Cheese snoring on my bed like a little old man. She rested a hand on her chest, and something harsh softened within her eyes. "I'll go to the pet store before Grandma finishes dinner."

I kissed Mami's cheek and whispered, "thank you," then closed the door so our new family member could sleep and dream about the wonders of his new life.

## CHAPTER 12: FIERY FLARE

The next morning, I groaned at the sound of my alarm, then turned over and smacked it. I didn't sleep all night, especially with the deep aches in my muscles. I shivered from the pain and tucked my blanket under my chin while Cheese kept my feet warm. Another wave of pain sent my nerves on fire, and I curled up like a dying bug. I closed my eyes and slept in a daze for the next few hours.

"*¿Mija, qué pasa*? It's twelve thirty!" Grandma touched my cheek, and my eyes creaked open.

"Flare day…not good."

"Mmmm." She kissed my forehead. "I'll bring you something to feel better. But at least get up and fix yourself, okay?"

I nodded and pushed myself up, feeling like I had the worst flu of my life. I shuffled into the bathroom with Cheese at my heels and looked down into his litter box. Poop! This confirmed my earlier suspicion that Cheese was a lost house cat.

"Good boy." I patted his butt and scratched his chin. Throughout the evening, Mami had obsessed over Cheese and watched him closely to see if he left us any "presents." After I brushed my teeth and washed my face, I put the bare amount of deodorant on so I wouldn't stink. I trudged back into bed and grabbed my phone. Nolia had passed by the lot and sent me before-and -after pics, since I forgot. Even though we still had some junk to clean up, my eyes widened. We had made amazing progress. I thought about creating a rough draft garden plan but sighed and closed my eyes.

Fiery flare days are always boring. Not only are you too exhausted to read or think, but it's even difficult to watch TV. Instead, I texted Nolia *thank you and good luck with your senior project today.* Nolia was starting her first day at the Art for Children organization.

I watched my favorite baking shows on my phone, then Grandma knocked on the door.

"Come in," I croaked.

"I made you chicken soup, and I brought aspirin and your special CBD oil."

"Thanks. Look at the pictures Nolia sent me."

She squinted at the screen through her glasses, and her eyebrows disappeared into her billowy hair puff. "Wow! No wonder you don't feel well. Even people without fibro would feel sore after all that work." She kissed my forehead. "And how is Tio?"

"He's good! Still into community service."

Grandma nodded, and she sighed. "It's a shame that your mami won't forgive him. Anyway, it's time to feed the little one." She scratched Cheese's hairy chin. *"¡Vamo, Queso!"*

When Grandma left the room, I burst out laughing at Cheese's bewildered expression and wide eyes. But when he heard Grandma open the cat food can, he ran out of the room with an excited meow. I grabbed my phone again while eating my soup and checked my messages.

*Hey ; ) hope you're doing okay!* texted Jayden.

I grinned. *So so. Wanna video chat?*

A few minutes later, Jayden's number and gorgeous face popped up on my phone. She was in bed also, lying around in a sports bra and sweats. I blushed.

"Feeling like crap too?" I asked.

Jayden smirked. "Nah, just having a lazy day. I'll probably work on my senior project later." Her smile vanished. "But you look pale. Everything okay?"

I laughed and rolled my eyes. "I'm the palest Puerto Rican up in this neighborhood. But no, not really. I'm having a flare from all the work yesterday."

Jayden nodded, and concern clouded her gorgeous blue eyes. "Do you want to talk about it?"

And I did. I let everything out.

How Papi died.

The terrible agony in my heart when the doctor had pronounced him dead.

And the nightmares about my family, how everyone's hearts explode at once and I don't know what to do. Jayden was silent, and for once, I appreciated someone listening instead of offering weightless condolences. Because sometimes, you just don't feel good and need to process it instead of shoving it in another room like Mami.

"Thank you for listening."

She smiled, but I still saw a trace of sadness. "I'm always here. Call me a little later when you feel better!" She puckered up and kissed the camera screen before hanging up.

I gripped my sheets and Cheese paced on the bed, sensing I was upset. Grandma knocked this time, and her face crumpled. She had heard everything. She rushed over to me with teary eyes, and we cried together, grief-filled sobs we had held in for way too long.

I slept the rest of the day and dreamed about Jayden and I kissing, or strange, disturbing visions, like my family suffocating. I was still too exhausted to keep my eyes open and process my pain. Sleeping was a better coping option. Toward dinner time, Cheese and I moped downstairs, where I ate in silence. Isi and Willie gave me lots of kisses, knowing that I was having a "sick day."

"Thank you, loves." I kissed each of their foreheads, and Grandma chased them into the living room so I could eat in peace.

Mami glared at me across the table. "Your hair is a mess and you're still in your nightclothes."

I shrugged. "Just having a bad fibro day from the cleanup." I smiled through my pain and showed her the pictures Nolia had sent me. She nodded but pointed to the back corner. "But you left some junk behind."

I slid my phone into my pocket and clenched my jaw. When I finished eating, I shuffled into the kitchen and grabbed the clean dishes to help Grandma. "No, Nichi. Have some tea instead and just relax, okay?"

Nodding, I brewed a strong cup of black tea and headed upstairs. Cheese spent time downstairs and played with his new toys. I smiled when Isi and Willie screech-laughed at his antics.

But a few moments later, Mami sighed as she walked into the kitchen. "You spoil her too much. She needs to learn how to push through."

"Stop that, Mari! Your daughter is sick, and you treat her like a lazy good-for-nothing!"

I shut my eyes and chased away the tears. I wanted to fly down the stairs and scream at Mami, tell her I'm doing my best, and why can't she ever say anything nice? Instead, I saved my energy and grabbed a blank piece of paper from my desk. I sketched my dream community garden, added raised beds here and there, then mapped out the vegetable plants. Anytime my attention faltered, I concentrated on the people who supported me instead of pointing out my flaws.

# CHAPTER 13: CARNIVAL THRILLS

The next few days passed in a blur, and I rushed to complete all my homework on Wednesday afternoon since Jayden asked me out for the Spring Carnival. I fluffed my black curls and surveyed my outfit in the mirror; cute without being over the top. I rolled my eyes at my nerves.

"It's a white t-shirt and jeans. Relax, girl," I muttered to myself. When I applied eyeliner, I stopped and remembered Monday morning when Jayden had snuck up behind me and kissed my cheek. I closed my eyes and savored the moment.

"Hi to you too." I kissed her and smiled. By now, news had spread that Jayden and I were a couple, and people stared when we showed affection.

She smirked and grabbed my hand. "Did you hear what's going on this week?"

"No, I've just been thinking about Cheese and the lot."

"There's a fair coming to the neighborhood in a few days. Do you wanna go with me?"

"Hmm." I tapped my chin and tried not to smirk. "Like a date?"

Jayden blushed and let out a nervous chuckle. "Jeez, you're killin' me."

"Of course, I'll go! Is seven okay?"

I had told Mami and Grandma later that day and they encouraged me to enjoy it, but come home by ten. When I heard a knock on the door, my stomach flopped, and I took a breath to steady my shaking hands.

"Hi, Jayden! I'll get Nichi for you," Grandma said. She hollered my name up the stairs and I rushed down but stopped suddenly when I took in Jayden. She wore a leather jacket, black t-shirt, and skater sneakers. I gulped to calm my nerves. *Please don't let me be too obvious,* I prayed to Gaia. Obviously, Jayden knew my feelings, but Mami and Grandma? To them, we were just friends.

Mami smiled and greeted Jayden with a wave. "Where's Nolia?"

"Oh— she's pretty busy with senior project. You know how she is."

Mami raised her eyebrow, and I could tell her B.S. meter detected something shady. "Well, remember what we said. Back by ten, especially since you have school tomorrow."

I grabbed my purse and keys, then kissed them bye. Once my apartment door was closed, I sighed and grabbed Jayden's hand.

She chuckled. "You okay?"

"Yeah, my mom's overbearing. I just want to have fun tonight and not think of them."

"Fair enough. How did Mrs. Perez react to the pics?"

"Great! She was surprised by the amount of work we accomplished. Plus, I sent her a draft of what I want to plant, so she'll forward everything to the City Council."

I also thought back to the moment Mrs. Perez had removed her thick, black-framed glasses and considered me with a proud smile. "You know, it makes me think of all the abandoned lots and space that we don't use wisely. I hope this project inspires our community to focus on green space."

I had to bite my lip to stop myself from crying and smiled.

As we walked the last few blocks to the carnival, I asked Jayden how their senior project was coming along. "It's good. I enjoy baking and want to pursue it as a career one day. I wanna make something for you. What's your favorite dessert?"

"You can't ask a curvy girl such a tough question. But to make it easier for you, anything chocolate!"

Jayden laughed. "I'll keep that in mind."

We rounded a corner and instead of the usual flea market that filled the massive parking lot, bright bursts of colorful light, screaming kids, and the delectable scent of fried food filled the air. Jayden paid for our tickets, then asked me to lead the way. But where do you start? There was a huge Ferris wheel, a roller coaster, and tons of games. But then my nose detected sugar, cinnamon, and hot oil.

"Wanna split a funnel cake?" Usually, the gluten killed my joints, but I didn't care that night.

"Hell yeah!"

Jayden gripped my hand, and we hurried up to the booth, but as I took out my wallet, she grasped my hand. "I brought money, too. Let's split it," I said.

She leaned in close to my ear. "Hell no. I'm spoiling my girl tonight."

I turned away and hid my goofy smile. Even though I've only had one secret boyfriend (because according to Mami, no dating without her permission) I was never treated to anything special. I practically floated behind Jayden to a sticky bench where we took turns ripping into the funnel cake. "This is perfect, you know? I mean, I hope you think so, too."

"What do you mean?"

"I don't know. A lot of girls like going on fancy dates, but I prefer casual, fun stuff. Is this okay?"

I stopped her hand from taking another bite. "This is perfect. Seriously. You don't need to do anything expensive with me. I know it sounds cheesy, but I just enjoy spending time with you."

Jayden's blue eyes locked onto my lips and kissed me. I desperately wanted to keep going, but kissing a girl in public, especially in my neighborhood, wasn't the best idea. "Okay, so rides or games first?" she asked.

"Games, because I have to show you what's up."

Jayden's eyes widened. "Oh really? Challenge accepted!"

With our hands entwined, we rushed over to a water gun gallery and this time, I insisted on paying. My adrenaline soared as the bell sounded for us to start. I'm not a competitive person, but carnival games are an Olympic sport for me. To my utter shock and embarrassment, Jayden beat me and laughed at my expression.

"Whatya want?" The carnival game operator gestured to a bunch of stuffed animal prizes hanging above the booth. Jayden sent me a sneaky glance, then pointed at the cartoony, orange-stuffed cat.

"That one, please."

He passed it down to them, and I gushed. "It's Cheese Two!" Then I kissed her cheek, and the challenge was on again. We bounced from one booth to another, collecting small plastic toys, and I won a gigantic stuffed alligator for Jayden. I checked my watch and sighed when I noticed it was a little after nine. "We only have time for one ride."

"How about the Ferris wheel?"

I *hate* heights, even in a slow-moving wheel. But I mustered up enough courage to say yes. We waited anxiously in line until we were strapped in and rolling forward. I gripped Jayden's hand, and she wrapped her arm around me.

We almost made a full turn when the ride stopped.

"Can I ask you something?"

Jayden shrugged. "Sure."

"Why do you like me?"

"What do you mean?"

"I'm overweight, not the prettiest girl in our grade, and my fibromyalgia causes a lot of problems. I feel like an old lady."

Jayden shook her head in disgust. "Who told you this?"

"Um, well...my mom points out my weight a lot—"

"This is why my dad and I moved away. My mom was hyper-critical of my dad. Said he didn't make enough money like everyone else on the block. And she hated I was 'confused.'" Jayden turned toward me. "Nich, I don't care what your mom says or what you think of yourself. I like you. You and Nolia are the only ones who've become my closest friends. Besides, you have a gorgeous smile, and I love that you're so caring and want to make a difference in your community. Should I keep going?"

"Sure," I laughed.

"We both love books and literature, which isn't common for teenagers nowadays, and we have similar music interests. I don't know how to describe it." Jayden shrugged. "I just felt this instant connection. We are friends at the core, but I see you as a beautiful girl who I want to share my life with."

The wheel started up again, and we admired the twinkling carnival lights in silence. Jayden smiled and put her arm around me. When we hopped off the Ferris wheel, I checked the time. "It's getting late, so let's head home."

But a cackling laugh destroyed our moment.

"Ew, who invited the lesbians to the fair?"

My blood boiled like hot oil. Talia.

"Seriously, this isn't the Pride Parade. These fags should get lost."

"I can't believe they kiss in public. It's disgusting!" one of her friends shouted.

Before Jayden spit a remark, I shoved my orange kitty at her, grabbed Talia's drink, and dumped orange soda all over her white dress.

Talia shrieked. "What the hell is wrong with you?"

But her friends covered their mouths and tried to stop laughing. I snatched her small glittery barrette and snapped it in half, then flung it behind me into the garbage. "*Never* call me a fag again, do you hear me? If you mess with me again, I'll break your nose."

Everyone around us stopped to stare, wondering if they should pull out their phones or call the cops. Instead, the crowd burst into hysterical laughter, and I recognized some kids from my school. They pulled out their phones, and Talia was finally in the flashing spotlight like she always wanted.

Jayden and I strutted away and headed around the corner. She stopped me against the wall and kissed me hard. "Now *that* was hot." I could've stood there all night, but we were dangerously close to curfew. A few blocks later, it was difficult to go our separate ways. I giggled under my breath. "You don't know the wrath of a Puerto Rican mom. Now go! I'll text you later."

Jayden kissed me again, then waved and headed down the block.

I looked at the time; ten fifteen. Cringing, I unlocked the door and Cheese meowed like a tattle-tale alarm. I sighed when Mami got off the couch.

"Didn't we say ten o'clock, Nilsa?"

"I know, I'm sorry. We got stuck on the Ferris wheel."

Mami sighed and rubbed her eyes. "Always excuses—" she stopped and stared at me. "Why are your cheeks so flushed? Are you drunk?"

"What? Are you kidding me? We went to the fair!"

Mami crossed her arms. "Nilsa, are you dating Jayden?"

"What is with the third degree, Mami? She's my friend, nothing more. I'm going to sleep."

But as I headed up the stairs with Cheese at my heels, I closed my eyes and felt a deep sense of shame.

---

When I was a little girl, Papi had taught me to love everyone, no matter their background, religion, race, or beliefs. "We need to create a more caring world, you understand?"

I nodded and turned back to the TV, some telenovela drama. Two women held hands and turned to kiss each other. My eyes widened. "Papi, girls don't kiss each other, right?"

Papi smiled at me. "It's okay, Nichi. Love comes in all different forms. Sometimes even two men fall in love—"

"What are you telling her?" Mami had stormed into the room and shut off the T.V. "Homosexuality is a *sin*, Chip." Mami reinforced that being gay was *asqueroso*, disgusting, and wasn't "right."

But Papi reminded me while growing up that love is love, and we needed more of it in a perilous world. And I didn't understand what the big deal was. I didn't care if someone kissed another person of the same gender.

But now I realized it *is* a big deal. I abandoned God and chose Gaia because I didn't question if she loved me.

Cheese interrupted my thoughts with a small purr and snuggled next to me. I scratched his chin, reflecting on his cunning nature, his strange similarities to Papi. I even wondered if he was a reincarnate of him. When the house was silent, I snuck into my closet again and changed the candles to a deep crimson.

"Thank you, Gaia, for this wonderful night of love and good fortune. I only pray that you will continue to lead me down the best path. Should I tell Mami about Jayden?" Cheese watched in fascination as I spoke to my idol, and then I made the sign of the pentagram and headed back into bed. My joints ached when I stretched my fingers, and Cheese licked me. My pain dissipated under his gentle touch, and I closed my eyes.

Love will always triumph and heal.

## CHAPTER 14: THE FIRST SEEDS

The next morning, when Nolia and I met up to head for school, I spilled the details. She spat out her hot coffee on the frosted sidewalk and squealed, which almost deafened me, but I smiled at her support. "Tell me everything!" As we continued walking, I told her about our first date at the fair, how Jayden asked me out on the Ferris wheel, and how Talia almost spoiled the night.

"Wow, that's some first date. I can't believe Talia! I never thought she was homophobic."

"I don't think she is. She just wants to ruin my life. But I have a feeling that from now on, she'll keep her mouth shut."

"Did you tell Mami yet?"

I opened my mouth to respond but couldn't think of a solid excuse.

"Nichi! You can't keep your relationship a secret forever."

"I know! But I also don't want to start a fight."

I shrugged to end the topic, but it came up later when I met Jayden in the hallway.

"Hey gorgeous." She wrapped her arm around me, and I pecked her cheek.

She tossed her black locks out of her face and blushed. "I was just wondering…have you told your mom about us?"

I bit my lip. "It's a bit…complicated. Mami is very religious."

Jayden grimaced. "I don't want you to be embarrassed of me."

"It's not you at all! Please don't think that." I kissed her cheek again and reached for her hand.

"All right, we'll figure it out together."

But even as she walked away, I sensed tension between us and knew we stalled the fight for another day.

---

Over the weekend, Jayden, Nolia, Tío Miguel, and I finished cleaning up the last junk and finally had an open space to plan the garden. Since it was still late February and heading into March, we couldn't plant anything yet. Otherwise, the frost would kill our seedlings. While we waited for the weather to warm up, Tío Miguel scoured lumberyards and his friends' backyards for clean, reclaimed wood and composite decking to build the raised planter beds.

The next few weeks went by without problems. Mami was unusually quiet and spent time by herself, and in school, people looked at me with newfound respect. Jayden and I kissed in the halls without rude stares ruining the moment, and Talia kept her distance. By April, we had unseasonably warm weather, and one Saturday, afternoon when Nolia was free, we headed to the lot. Jayden had to work at the bakery for her senior project, which was a bummer.

Tío had delayed making the boxes because of other demands with community service. But now that the frosty weather melted away, we considered what to plant.

Nolia sipped on an iced coffee as we walked down the block. While we had kept in touch regularly, our senior projects had interrupted major girl time, so it was nice to catch up. "How's everything?" I asked.

"Good! Same old. I, uh, still haven't told Mami yet."

She shook her head. "Nichi, it's been like 3 months! That's going to cause problems in your relationship. Better fess up soon."

I sighed and shrugged.

Nolia took a loud slurp and shook the ice to find a few more sips. I was so jealous of her drink, especially since I was already sweating. She wore sunglasses on that day to hide her exhaustion, but when I brought it up, she shrugged it off. "Don't worry about it. It's just a lot to juggle, you know? Oh, I forgot to ask! How's Mr. Cheese doing?"

I burst out laughing at the name. "He's doing fantastic. In typical cat style, he thinks he owns the place, and Grandma always tells him to pay rent." I pulled out my phone and shared the thousands of photos I took during the last few months, from playful moments with toys, to sleeping positions, and catching a pic mid-yawn.

When we made it to the lot, Tío and his friends were building the garden beds of reclaimed wood and decking, just like he promised. The sound of power tools and hammering made me wince, but once I took in my project coming alive, I rushed up to Tío and planted a kiss on his sweaty bald head. "This looks amazing!" I screamed over the humming of an electric saw. Tío laughed and dumped a bunch of mulch to line one of the garden beds.

"It's the least I could do, Nich. We'll start putting healthy soil in by the afternoon."

I crossed my arms. "Tío, this is becoming an expensive project. Are you sure you don't want any money?"

Tío shook his head. "No, *mija*. Mr. Carlos at the hardware store bought a pallet of good soil to get us started. He was sick of this old eyesore too and wanted to contribute. Plus, your papi was his best customer, so it was the least he could do."

I nodded in silence.

"But hey, why don't you go buy some plants with your friend? There's a great nursery on Long Island. It's a decent bus trip, so here's some money—"

"No, no. Seriously, Tio, you did enough! I still have the money from the bake sale, remember?"

"Okay, be careful, sweetheart. We'll see you soon." Tío Miguel went back to work while Nolia and I hurried to catch the next bus.

"What do you want to plant, Nich?" Nolia looked over my shoulder at my extensive shopping list and garden plan that included tomatoes, cilantro, herbs, peppers, beans, and other vegetables commonly used in Latin cooking.

"Only the freshest ingredients for this community!"

The bus ride to Long Island was sweltering and crowded. I internally groaned when I had to peel my thighs off the vinyl seating, but Nolia didn't seem affected. "Damn, it's so hot! And it's only the beginning of April. Aren't you sweating?"

She shrugged. "A little. It's probably global warming. It's only downhill from here unless we do something."

I hadn't thought of that, and I suddenly felt trapped in the bus. As the temperatures gradually grew warmer over time, how would it affect inner-city communities? Would we bake to death between the buildings?

During the bus ride, Nolia and I discussed different ideas for our senior project, but because it was so hot, we tried to occupy ourselves by scrolling through our phones or listening to music. The first thing I promised to buy was a giant water bottle that we could split.

An hour and a half later, we arrived in a small Nassau County city with cookie-cutter houses and the lushest maple trees I've ever seen in a neighborhood. The nursery was down the block from the bus stop, and we trudged on in silence, wiping our foreheads. Like any busy city, cars honked, there was traffic, and plenty of people enjoying the weather. But once we stepped through the nursery gates, everything became peaceful, as if we left the city world behind us. Birdsong replaced the annoying din of traffic, and chubby bumblebees buzzed along colorful flowers.

A variety of plants were spread across a sprawling lot, ranging from ornate roses to shrubbery and mounding perennial flowers. Another part of the nursery had garden décor, like fancy statues and ponds, but we skipped it entirely. I wanted to keep our community garden practical. As we headed further into the nursery, the quieter it became, and I suddenly imagined Jayden and I having a house there. Could we build a life together after college? I stared across the street at one of the small houses with just enough green space to build a garden. I pictured us lounging outside with iced drinks, and a feeling of content washed over me.

"Nich, you okay?" Nolia patted my arm and handed me a water bottle she bought at the nursery register.

"Mhm." The vision disappeared. I had learned after Papi died that you can't predict the future and expect it to work out like perfect puzzle pieces. Sometimes, a piece gets lost or damaged, and you just have to focus on present issues.

An older woman with a worn baseball cap and a green nursery t-shirt strolled up to us. She reminded me of Grandma with her warm smile. "Can I help you ladies?"

"Yes! I'm working on a community garden, and I'd like to see your vegetable plants."

She grinned. "Sure! Are there specific plants you're looking for?"

"Since we live in a Latin neighborhood, I want everyone to have the freshest ingredients for the food we usually cook, so peppers, both spicy and sweet, tomatoes, beans, maybe zucchini..."

"Since there is still a possibility of frost at night, start your seedlings indoors. If you plant anything now, it may get destroyed. Follow me." We passed by a variety of small buildings until we stepped into a cramped open shack that had kitschy garden décor, decorative stones with quotes, and display tables full of seeds.

I listed the plants off on my fingers and she passed me each packet. "Oh! Thank you."

"Any herbs?"

"Cilantro is a must, along with oregano, parsley, and mint."

The woman rotated a display carousel, pulling out the little envelopes and handed them to me with a smile. "Now, these are good to get you started, but you also want to attract pollinators, like bees and butterflies. They'll help your produce develop."

"I hadn't thought of that." While I had considered my people, what about the other creatures that called the city home? I'm sure there weren't enough plants to keep large populations of bees happy and thriving. My eyes widened; I couldn't remember the last time I saw a butterfly. "What are some plants that are easy to maintain but still attract pollinators?"

"Well, planting the herbs is a good start, but adding some echinacea, bee balm, and milkweed is great! Echinacea is also known as purple coneflower and is used as an herbal remedy. Bee balm is a great remedy too, but milkweed is especially important. It's the only plants that monarch butterflies will lay their eggs on. Unfortunately, because everyone and their grandmother uses pesticides, the monarchs are slowly dying off, so planting as much milkweed as possible is crucial."

She passed us the echinacea and bee balm seed packets, but I didn't see the milkweed. "I have them back here." She walked us to another section of the nursery where butterflies of all colors and shapes fluttered about like fairies. "They're beautiful!" Nolia whispered. A curious yellow one with big spots landed on her arm, and she laughed when it tickled her.

The woman smiled. "That's a swallowtail, one of my favorites. All of them are particularly attracted to this butterfly bush, but I only recommend this to people who have a lot of yard space. It gets huge. But here is the milkweed!"

She pulled out two pots with an ordinary-looking plant. "It doesn't look like much, but once the weather warms up, it has these beautiful small blooms. I'm selling them at a discount, too."

"We'll take them."

"Is that everything for you ladies?"

"Yes but, I have no idea how to start seeds indoors."

She smiled. "Oh, that's not a problem!" Then we walked with her to another portion of the nursery where there were bottles of organic fertilizers and small trays. "All you need is some good soil. Avoid using anything labeled topsoil since it's not nutrient-dense. Then, add a little soil into each cell." She picked up a tray and pointed to little cardboard containers. "This is peat moss, so it will naturally degrade once you add it to your garden. Make sure the earth is moist but not wet and keep it near a sunny window. Once your seedlings sprout, it's best to plant them immediately. Otherwise, they'll get "leggy" which means they stretch too far and fall over."

"What else can you use for planters?"

"Pretty much anything! As long as it can't grow mold like paper or cardboard and drains properly."

Nolia and I nodded at each other. "This should be it. Thank you so much for your help."

The woman smiled and led us inside the main building to a cashier. She rang everything up and placed our supplies in paper bags.

Sweat trickled down my spine. What if I didn't have enough? I knew the seeds were cheap, but I didn't add up the milkweed, fertilizer, and planting cells.

"Excuse me, ma'am. I know you helped us a great deal, but I'm wondering if I can ask you for a favor." I pulled out the official letter from the city. "I'm working on this garden for my community as a senior project. Is there any way I get a student discount?" I squeaked out my last question. Nolia nudged my ribs, believing I was pushing my luck.

For a moment, she looked at me, then examined the letter. "Well, I— that's incredible. I am truly moved." She gulped for a second and shook her head. "Sorry, I don't mean to get emotional on you. I've never seen young people so dedicated to creating safe natural environments. I'll give you half off everything, and the milkweed is free."

"Thank you—"

"But only if you come back and show me pictures when everything's set up. Deal?" She smiled.

"Absolutely! Thank you again, ma'am!"

"Call me Linda."

She placed the rest of our purchases in another bag and handed Nolia the milkweed. We promised to visit her soon and buy more plants. "Oh, I'm definitely coming back here once I get my license. Did you see how gorgeous the butterflies were? It would be a shame if monarchs died out," Nolia said.

Even though we had spent one hundred fifty dollars, and I was worried about other costs, my eyes teared up and I wrapped an arm around my best friend. When we boarded the bus, Nolia offered to pay the fare this time. On the way home, she researched butterflies on her phone, showing me the most beautiful species in New York like swallowtails, regal moths, and common buckeyes. Soon the peaceful suburbs turned into city skyscrapers and loud, hectic traffic, and I thought about how much the community supported my project, even those who were strangers.

"Nichi! Look at this one!" Nolia pointed to another butterfly picture and beamed.

And I realized that once somebody experiences the beauty of nature, there was no turning your back on Her.

## CHAPTER 15: EL PLANTON

"Look at my little babies!" I squealed over the rows of seedlings stretching toward the sun. I gently touched one of the pepper leaves. Cheese ran into my bedroom meowing like crazy and zig-zagged between my legs.

"Cheese! I was talking to the plants, not you!" I picked him up and kissed his forehead, then set him down on my bed. It was difficult keeping Cheese's curiosity away from the plants, like it was his instinct to chew them. So, Grandma bought him a cat grass plant when she went to buy him more food.

I thought back to a few weeks ago when Nolia and I had planted the milkweed by the herbal section and anxiously waited for the fresh blooms to attract butterflies. For the seeds, we followed Linda's instructions and scooped dirt from the raised beds and filled the peat moss cells. Then we carefully labeled each one so we wouldn't confuse the seedlings. I didn't know seeds were like babies; they needed constant care and a delicate touch. Some needed only a little light, some needed full sunshine, and some preferred shade. When we had finished, we high-fived each other and were about to set them near my bedroom window. Mami had come outside to check on our progress and noticed soil on the steps. She pointed a manicured finger at the dirt. "Clean that up when you're done," she said and closed the door.

Nolia had rolled her eyes. "Jeez." I shrugged and ignored Mami's comment. We set up a small folding table under my bedroom window and placed the cells directly in the sun.

Now, we had to get the plants into the soil before they became "leggy" as Linda described. I fluffed my black curls and checked myself over once more. Jayden was coming over to help me plant, and it had been a while since we caught up. Sure, she was my girlfriend, but the senior project was taking up most of our time. When the doorbell rang, I headed downstairs. "I'll get it!"

I opened the door and grinned at Jayden. She smiled but made no effort to kiss me, especially with Mami looming in the background.

"Hey! How's the plants?"

"They look great! I can't wait to see how big they grow in a few weeks, especially now that it's optimal plant time."

Jayden stepped inside and gave Grandma a big hug but waved cautiously to Mami. "Hello."

"Hi, Jayden. I'll let you two work on the project. Oh, and Nichi, keep the door open."

I gulped but didn't say anything. Mami hadn't said that since I had dated a boy last year before Papi died. Were my feelings too obvious? Jayden and I remained silent as we took the seedlings outside and headed down the block to the garden.

"That was weird."

"You mean your mom?"

"Yeah...I still haven't said anything."

Jayden sighed and avoided my eyes. As we turned the corner, I still couldn't believe how much work we completed in just a few months. Beautiful wooden raised beds, all filled with nutritious black soil replaced the decrepit garbage. The beds were arranged in a big U shape, the biggest one for vegetables while the other two were for herbs and pollinator plants. Paved steppingstones surrounded each bed for easy access and to keep the grass maintenance low. I was amazed by the congregation of birds that perched around the surrounding buildings, watching our progress like anxious sentinels. I mentally reminded myself to buy a bird feeder and bath once everything else was finished. I smiled at Jayden as I passed her a pair of gardening gloves. She was still quiet, and my stomach dropped in dread.

"Just tell me where each plant needs to go."

"Right." I started breaking apart the tomato cells and instructed Jayden how each one should be placed. Even though we were silent, I focused on the soil running through my fingers, the scent of damp earth, and giving back to Gaia. It took us some time to finish the vegetables, and then we moved onto the next bed. By midday, I was exhausted and out of breath. Sweat trickled down my underarms and breasts, but I didn't care. Yes, the work was physically demanding, especially in the sun, but seeing how the garden developed over the last few months, especially with plants, made my heart swell with pride. I had hoped the community would recognize our efforts and take care of it, too.

Jayden sighed as she planted the last cilantro seedling and sat back to rest. "Nich, we need to talk."

My heartbeat sped up. "Okay." I sat down next to her.

"Why haven't you told your mom yet?"

"I—"

"We've been together for almost six months!"

I sighed in frustration. "Jayden, it's not that simple. Most Spanish parents are *very* strict with their children. Ever since Papi died, Mami has kept me locked up. I can't date, have to be home early, and if I'm not, a fight starts. Plus, she's not exactly on the rainbow train... if you know what I mean."

"Oh, great," Jayden huffed.

"I promise to tell her one day, but lately, I'm walking on eggshells and don't want to start World War Three in my house, okay?"

She nodded. "I'm sorry. I guess I've been so excited that I forgot about your perspective."

"No, no. *I'm* sorry. I just want you to know that I'm not trying to hide you. Can we make up?"

Jayden rolled her eyes and smiled. "We weren't fighting."

"Yes, we were!"

"Now we are!"

We both burst into laughter and kissed each other. "Come on, let's finish up so we can relax in the air conditioning," I said. Jayden and I added the last row of mint seedlings and made sure to keep them separate from the rest of the plants. "It grows wild," Linda had reminded me, "and needs constant maintenance." I stopped for a moment. Just like a garden, relationships require effort and work, no matter if it's your mother or partner. I silently promised that I would break the news at dinner tonight.

"Wow, this place looks awesome!" I recognized Tío Miguel's booming voice and turned to smile through my exhaustion. "Thanks, Tio. I couldn't have done it without you— or you, Jayden." I gripped her hand and kissed her cheek.

"I brought you something to honor your papi." Tío held up a terra cotta pot, and inside was the beginning stages of a hosta plant, his favorite. I covered my mouth and tears stung my eyes. "Aww, Nich," Jayden hugged me, and I couldn't hold back anymore. "I miss him so much," my voice cracked, and I gently held the plant. Tears blurred my vision as I dug a hole big enough for the hosta and covered the roots with soil. A few tears landed on the gentle flower, and I struggled to hold back my sobs. Tío rubbed my back while Jayden kissed my tear-soaked cheeks. With a final struggle of breath, I pushed myself off the ground. "Now he's always with us."

But my stomach dropped to Hell when Mami rounded the corner. I watched her eyes widen in shock, then her face contorted in rage. "Nilsa!" she hissed. "I—can't believe this! I stopped by to check on your progress and you're with *him?*" She pointed at Tío like he was dog shit on the pavement.

Tío held his hands up. "I was just helping. That's all."

"*Helping*? By teaching Nilsa how to abandon her family? How to get into jail and the best gangs?"

"Mami!"

Tío closed his eyes and clenched his jaw. "I'm leaving. You won't see me again."

"No, Tío!" But he headed back to his car and didn't turn to look at me.

Mami's hawk eyes swiveled back to me. "Come home right now. You're telling me everything."

I shot Jayden an apologetic glance and followed Mami around the corner, mentally bracing myself for the upcoming battle.

# CHAPTER 16: FUEGO

Mami had controlled herself the entire walk home, but I watched the way her muscles tensed, her hands bunching into fists. When we got back to the apartment, she slammed the door, and the walls quaked.

"What in the hell is going on, Nilsa? Why have you been working with Tío behind my back?"

I trembled and finally faced her. "Because of *you!* You hate him for mistakes he made in the past. He's family, Mami. How could you?"

Grandma shuffled down the stairs in her *chanclas* and stood between us with her hands on her hips. "Mari, I've been telling you to move on for years."

"This doesn't involve you, Mother!"

"The hell it does! He's my son and you treat him like *mierta*! You treat your daughter just as bad!"

Upstairs, Willie and Isi cried at our raised voices, and Cheese ran to them.

"I'll raise my daughter how I want to! You are *not* her mother!"

I stepped in front of Grandma, almost nose to nose with Mami. "Don't talk to her like that! You're always pushing everyone away or forcing people to bend, but I won't stop seeing my tío. He's the one who supported me, built the garden beds, and funded most of my project, not you! You never helped or support me!"

"What are you talking about? I told you how proud I was."

"No, Mami. It doesn't work like that. You don't get to tell me *once* that you're proud and shit over everything else!"

Don't talk to me like that, Nilsa—"

"I'm sick of you always commenting on my health, how I never push through, and my weight. Do you know how *shitty* that makes me feel?" My voice cracked as tears blurred my vision.

Mami's eyes flared like the devil about to unleash hell on the world. "And you know what disgusts me the most? That you're dating a girl."

I stopped crying and swallowed my tears. "That's none of your business."

"So, you going against God and what I say is not my business? It's disgusting, Nilsa! You need to break it off today—"

"I miss Papi more than I love you!"

We raged at each other and screamed until our throats burned. But when Mami raised her ringed hand and slapped my face, I stumbled back. But all fear of my mother vanished, instead turning into vile rage. I screamed and lunged for her, but Grandma grabbed my waist.

"No, don't—!"

"You *BITCH!*"

Grandma released my waist and gasped. Mami's eyebrows disappeared into her black hairline, and she trembled. "That's it. Get out and don't come home." She pointed her red fingernail at the door.

"Whatever." I stomped upstairs and packed a bag for the night. Before I left, I stopped in front of Grandma and stared into her heartbroken eyes. "Take care of Cheese for me."

Then I slammed my apartment door without a single glance back at Mami and headed for Nolia's place. When I crossed the street, I stood in front of the door, my knocking turning into furious pounding with tears of vile anger blurring my eyes.

When she unlocked the door, Nolia noticed my trembling and held her arms out, the one savior I needed in this sickening situation. I sobbed into her open arms, and she pulled me inside.

## CHAPTER 17: MY "PERFECT" FAMILY

Days later, I was still at Nolia's house, feeling like an imposing lump in the spare room. I sighed, missing my lavender comforter and my pink walls, my cluttered vanity and stacks of books. Here, the room was a bland beige, like a hotel. Still, I was grateful for Nolia and her mother, Bernice. That night, I had broken down and explained everything to Bernice, how Mami had lost it since Papi passed away, and she hated me for dating Jayden. She shook her head and hugged me. She smelled like rose soap and *sazón*. "Honey, you stay here as long as you need to. Your momma should know better." Bernice's large golden hoop earrings as she shook her head. "The only thing that matters is your heart is full of love."

Once I showered and changed into comfortable clothes, Nolia pulled down the bedsheets for me. I groaned as I rolled over as she lay next to me.

"Nich, you're not looking good." She put a hand on my forehead.

"It's a bad flare, Nols." I must've fallen asleep because when I woke up in the middle of the night, the room was dark, and Nolia was in her room.

The next morning, Bernice made us gluten-free pancakes and scrambled eggs, a welcoming breakfast after a horrible night of sleeplessness. I had thought about the argument with Mami all night. I had missed three days of school, and Nolia gave me a daily stack of homework that I set aside.

Grandma called me the next night via video chat. I could tell she had been crying, but just like all the women in our family, she smiled through her pain. "You look tired, *mija*."

I desperately tried to keep my eyes open. "Yeah, it's been rough."

She sighed and paused for a moment. "*Mija*, you know I love you, and I spoke to Mami about smacking you, but calling her a bitch was—"

"I know."

Now, the number one rule in any Spanish household is *never ever*, not even if your life is in danger and the world is about to explode, call your mami a bitch. To this day, she still brings it up in arguments. But even though I was out of line, I couldn't take it anymore, and for her to disown me over my sexuality broke my heart.

"You know I love you, no matter what?"

"Mhm." I covered my mouth when tears spilled down my cheeks.

"I'm serious, Nilsa. Whether you're gay, straight, or figuring it out, you are my granddaughter, and I will always love you. And I believe Mami loves you, too. She just…she needs time."

Grandma tried to lighten the mood by turning the camera toward Cheese, who sat on the couch next to her. She baby-talked him, and he let out an exaggerated meow. I laughed through my tears until I couldn't stop.

"Well, I guess a smile is better than crying," Grandma chuckled. "I'm going to talk to Mami today. You'll come home soon, no?"

I nodded.

"All right. *Te quiero, mija.*" She blew a kiss into the phone before hanging up.

After the phone call, Nolia knocked on the spare bedroom door and peaked inside. "How's Abuelita?"

"Good." Pain wracked my nerves, and I groaned through my teeth.

"Oh, Nichi." Nolia sat down beside me and wrapped her arms around my shoulders.

"Ow!" I cried again as agony spread through my neck muscles, like tender skin or body aches from the flu. She patted the bed and tucked me in. "I'll get you some aspirin. In the meantime, someone is here to see you."

I closed my eyes and braced for Mami's harsh eyes, but two beautiful blue ones greeted me instead. "Nich, oh God. Nolia told me everything, and I had to see you. It's all my fault!" Jayden cried. She ran a hand through the longer side of her hair. I know she was panicking, but damn if I wasn't flaring in that moment…

I shook my head. "No, Jayden. This is just my family."

She cradled me in her loving embrace, rocking me gently until I almost fell asleep on her chest. Nolia joined us and sat at the edge.

"Nichi, you have to confront your mother," Jayden said.

"I agree," Nolia said. "Your mom needs to accept you, or that's it. And even if she still gives you a problem, we're here for you, girl."

I wiped my eyes, took a deep breath, and grabbed my phone.

*Mami, we need to talk.*

A few minutes later, my phone buzzed with a reply. *Come home tonight.*

# CHAPTER 18: NUESTRO CORAZONES

The next afternoon, I packed my bags and fixed myself up, always desperate to live up to Mami's standards. It had been days since I brushed my hair or wore a pair of jeans, and I felt like my old self. Before I left Nolia's house, I took a deep breath. She stood next to me and grabbed my hand.

"You're not alone. Jayden and I are going to be there, remember?"

I nodded and took another breath to steady my nerves. After I had received Mami's text, I immediately called Grandma and told her everyone needs to share their perspective, and she agreed. We crossed the street and unlocked my apartment door. Grandma bear-hugged both of us with tears in her eyes, and Cheese zig-zagged around my ankles, meowing like I had a tasty bag of treats in hand. I patted and shushed him gently. "I'm here, baby." I stood up and sighed, wiping a hand over my face.

"We're going to get through this, Nilsa. I promise." Grandma held my tear-stained face and kissed my cheeks. Once I settled in and unpacked my stuff, Jayden knocked on the door. Together, we waited for half an hour in the living room until Mami finally came home. Like usual, she kicked off her heels, exhaled a long sigh, then stopped when she noticed us in the living room.

"What's going on here?"

"We're having a family meeting," Grandma said.

Mami put her hands on her hips. "Then why are Jayden and Nolia here?"

"Because they're part of my family," I said and locked eyes with her.

Mami fixed her dress blouse and sat down on the opposite couch. "Okay, so where do we start?"

I cleared my throat, then grabbed Jayden and Nolia's hands. "Mami, I hate saying this to you, but ever since Papi died, you've become a nasty woman. I've done nothing to break your trust, but you question everything I do. You've also been very unsupportive with my gardening project, and I don't understand why you're nitpicking everything. I'm doing my best, even with my worst flare days. Don't you see that?"

"It's true, Mari," Grandma added. "I hear the way you talk to her, and it pushes Nilsa away. She always comes to me for support, like when she needed help during the bake sale."

Mami crossed her arms and pursed her lips.

"And also, Mrs. Rivera, it's not right that you pick on Nichi's weight, given that she has a disability and limited mobility," Nolia said. "Granted, she doesn't let this stop her, but she's always self-conscious of how she looks instead of seeing her beauty!"

Grandma raised her hands in exasperation. "And I didn't raise you to be homophobic. Even your husband used to say, 'love is love.' Where did this hate come from?"

Mami sat like a weathered stone, unmoving and stoic. But then her lip trembled, and tears streamed down her face. "Nilsa, I—I only want the best for you. I just wanted you to have a normal, good life, but everything became so hard—" She covered her mouth to stifle a sob.

"I'm sorry, Nilsa! I am so sorry for pushing you away. Ever since your papi died, I felt as if I needed to be a stricter parent, like I had to take on both roles, and I'm always so angry. Why didn't he listen to us about taking care of himself? How could he leave us so early?" She covered her face and sobbed. Everyone moved to the opposite couch to cradle her in a big hug.

"Mami, you need to talk to us. I'm still grieving too, and so is Grandma. It's okay to share your feelings. It's not a weakness!"

"You're right, I know. I just can't process that the love of my life is *gone*." She rocked back and forth, finally letting out her agonizing sobs. I cradled her face and wiped her eyes.

"Mami, we are going to get through this, but we have to see a family therapist. And Jayden is my girlfriend," I reached over to grab their hand. "I'm seventeen years old, and I can make my own decisions. Sure, we may face some hate, but being bisexual is *not* disgusting. You need to accept me the way I am."

Mami nodded and gripped my hand. "I understand, and please know from the bottom of my heart, how sorry I am to treat you both that way. I had this vision of a perfect daughter, like the American dream. But you are perfect, my darling girl. Your happiness is all that matters to me, baby." She held her arms open, and I didn't hesitate to hug her back and kiss her tears away. Once we all settled down, Grandma wiped her eyes.

"I should get started on dinner. Nolia and Jayden, will you stay with us?"

They nodded but turned to Mami for approval. "Yes, you both can stay. Family sticks together." She grabbed them in a big hug and kissed their cheeks.

"I could use some help in the kitchen!" Grandma called out.

"Coming, Abuelita!" Nolia ran into the kitchen while Jayden and I hung out on the couch. We must've fallen asleep from emotional exhaustion because when Mami announced dinner was ready, we pushed ourselves up and yawned. That night, Grandma and Nolia had created a feast of roast chicken, yellow rice, beans, and salad. My mouth watered at the aromas of garlic, cilantro, and delectable spices. Just as we sat down, someone knocked on the door.

"I'll get it," I said.

When I opened it, my stomach dropped. Tío Miguel stood there with a flower bouquet. "Grandma invited me over. Is that okay?"

I grinned. "Come in! We were just about to eat."

When Tío stepped through the door, everyone was quiet. Our eyes darted from Mami to Tio, back and forth to see who would make the first move. Tío held the flowers out to her.

She gripped him in a tight embrace, and they cried. Each whispered to one another how sorry they were for past mistakes and shutting each other out. Then, we said grace and dug into our meal. Mami and I exchanged glances; we had forgotten about Papi's chair, but in this moment, it was okay to give up our mournful shrine. Our laughter was the music, our stories the thread that held us together.

This is what Nuyorican culture is about. It doesn't matter what skin color you're born with, whether you're straight or gay or if you speak fluent Spanish. Boricua life is about family: sharing your love, pain, and experiences, then finding common ground over the dinner table.

# CHAPTER 19: PAPI'S MEMORY

The next morning, Tío called us during breakfast and said we needed to meet him at the community garden within an hour. He had a big surprise for us. Grandma rushed us to finish our eggs, and Mami got the kids ready.

Jayden and Nolia met us at the lot, and finally, Tío Miguel's old truck rumbled down the street. The sun had crept over the buildings, creating a warm golden haze. Tío Miguel smiled as he unloaded an enormous piece of wood. "The garden looks great, but it's missing one last piece to tie everything together. Close your eyes."

I gripped Jayden and Nolia's hands, then shut my eyes.

"One, two, three!"

We opened our eyes, and Tío turned the sign around. Mami and Grandma gasped, and I almost fell to my knees.

*In honor of Chip Sandford. Hero to this community and guardian of this space named, "Papi's Garden."*

The words were burned into the wood, creating burnished art alongside delicately crafted plant vines and flowers.

"It's beautiful," my voice cracked.

Tío looked down at his feet and sniffled. "I made it myself. Learned some skills over the years." He turned toward Mami, who embraced him and cried onto his shoulder.

We all stood together in silence as Tío Miguel hung the sign up on a wooden frame over my garden— *our* garden. We stood under the sign and cried, our sniffles the only hymn to Papi's memory. And I realized that if our community honored this space, Papi would always be with us.

## CHAPTER 20: MY FUTURE

A month later, when the weather turned humid and the promise of summer approached, Mami, Grandma, and I held a grand opening for the community garden. Everything had bloomed small white and yellow flowers, a promise of fresh food. A few of the tomato plants had budded tiny green spheres, and little beans hung safely under their guardian plant's leaves.

All my neighbors joined us for a garden party and admired my work. "Nena, I can't believe this! The space looks beautiful!" Mrs. Martinez, one of my older neighbors said. Linda the gardener had driven all the way from Long Island to attend our party, and she wiped her eyes. "My goodness, Nilsa. This is incredible!"

"I couldn't have done all of this without your guidance." I hugged her, and then greeted some of the other sponsors who helped make this dream a reality, like Tio's boss, Mr. Carlos, who was Papi's friend. His bushy gray eyebrows knotted together, and his eyes welled up. "You know, your father would be damn proud of this."

I nodded and bit my lip. But this time, instead of sadness, my heart swelled with joy.

Nolia and Bernice showed up with homemade empanadas, Tío Miguel brought beer and iced tea, and my girlfriend, the most beautiful, blue-eyed angel, baked two dozen of her famous chocolate hazelnut cupcakes. When I first bit into the moist sponge, my eyes rolled back, and I shook my head. "I don't care what you say babe, you're going to be on Food Network one day."

Jayden laughed at the comment and kissed my cheek. "Let's work on getting our degrees first!"

Along the outer edge of the garden, Mami, Tio, and Grandma each held a cold beer and laughed, reminiscing home memories with tears in their eyes.

"Let's turn the salsa up!" Mr. Jimenez, the corner store owner, shouted over the crowd. Tío went into his car and blasted the local Latin channel, and we all danced to our favorite salsa and meringue hits, which drew even more people to join us.

Nolia, Jayden, and I parted from the crowd to talk among ourselves. The senior project fair was in a few days. "So, what are your plans for school?" I asked.

"Graphic design. The place I interned at this semester wants to hire me part time while I apply for schools!" Nolia grinned.

Jayden shrugged. "For now, I'll work on the local bakeries over the summer and see what culinary arts programs are offered at different schools in the area."

I smiled and nodded, happy that two of my best friends had a bright future.

But inside, my stomach rolled in panic. I had no idea what to pursue for a future career.

---

The school gym buzzed with excitement and was packed with senior students showing off their hard work this semester. Everyone had fancy screens to showcase slideshows or posterboards full of collages. I took the easier route and chose a poster since I was still tending the garden and catching up on late work. But my hands trembled like crazy, especially when I learned that college recruiters had attended to see who was the best fit for their top programs. Honestly, I expected people to pass my booth or laugh at me, but a crowd had gathered to check out my work and were totally impressed with the before-and-after pictures. Talia sulked at her empty booth on the other side of the gym, and I held back a giggle. I turned my attention back to the growing crowd.

"Even though we live in a city, it's important to maintain our green spaces so we can have easy access to fresh food and healthier environments. Studies show that green spaces reduce stress and attract a myriad of important animals." I also explained how easy it was to start a garden in a minimal amount of space along with the best soil practices for future generations.

"For example, in front of me is a free sample of fresh salsa I made with the tomatoes, cilantro, and peppers I grew in the community garden. Enjoy!"

Like swarming bees, people nudged one another to taste my food and nodded enthusiastically at the blended flavors.

"I taste the difference in this," someone commented.

"Can I get the recipe?"

"I need step-by-step instructions on how to grow plants!"

I passed around a small packet covering the basics of my presentation. Eventually, everyone shuffled off, and then Mrs. Perez and the Senior Project Council stepped up to my booth. "We just heard your presentation, Nilsa. Fantastic work!" Mrs. Perez said.

One woman with frizzy red hair and thick blue glasses, whom I later learned was a part of City Council, smiled at me. "We were worried about this project given the amount of work. You should be so proud of your efforts, Miss Rivera!"

I blushed at their praise. "Oh, I—thank you!"

Mrs. Perez marked something down on a clipboard and stepped down to the next booth. In the background, a stout younger black woman waved to me and approached my table. She wore a finely tailored gray suit. Her thick braids were styled in a neat bun. "Hi there! My name is Aimee, and I'm an academic recruiter for The Horticulture University of Long Island. After seeing your presentation, we believe you are an excellent candidate for one of our programs. Here, take my card!" Aimee gave me her contact information, and my heart raced with excitement.

I grinned and shook her hand. "When do you need the application by?"

"Preferably before summer break. We hope to hear from you!"

When Aimee said goodbye and searched for more students, I finally had a clear vision for my future. Whenever my hands dug into the soil, raised seedlings, or studied hard at the University, Papi would be right behind me, whispering words of encouragement.

# EPILOGUE

I review the last words of my essay and nod in acceptance. "Yay! Finally!" I squeak. Summer is officially here, and I hurry to submit my essay in the online academic portal. After I told Mrs. Perez about the academic recruiter, she promised to keep in touch. She and Mami go out to lunch often, so I know she'll become a member of our growing family.

I rush to grab my first-ever two-piece swimsuit, then pull on my shorts and a tank top. The swimsuit is bright aqua blue that shows enough skin and curves to make me feel sexy. Nolia, Jayden, and I planned this trip to Long Island to celebrate and enjoy the beach waves before college started in late August. I hadn't visited the beach since Papi was alive. But his memory no longer brings sadness to my heart, and my tears finally dried. Every time I think about him, my heart swells with pride. Because he shared his love of gardening with me, I found my passion.

"Nilsa! Jayden and Nolia are here!" Grandma calls from downstairs.

"Coming!" I give Cheese a big kiss. "See you later, buddy!" He closes his eyes and resumes napping.

When I enter the kitchen, Grandma passes me a small cooler. "Here, I packed you some sandwiches and cold *malta*. Be careful and enjoy yourselves!"

Mami stands at the door with Nolia and Jayden. Even after a few weeks of family therapy, I see a tremendous change in her demeanor. Her shoulders no longer slump as if she's carrying Papi's death by herself, and she can't stop smiling.

"Do you have sunscreen?"

I check my bag. "Yup!"

"Your aspirin?"

"Uh, yes."

"What about—"

"Mami, I'll be okay."

She hugs me, and I squeeze her. "Love you."

"I love you too, baby. Have fun."

Nolia, Jayden, and I laugh in excitement as we hop into Nolia's new car she received for graduation. Mami promised I would get a car before college, especially since my application for the horticulture program was accepted.

"Can we swing by the garden for just a minute? I just need to check—"

Jayden groans and Nolia leans over the front seat. "Didn't we agree to have a fun-filled day with no work?"

"I'll make it quick. I promise."

Nolia grumbles as we drive around the block, and to my surprise, the community is busy pruning, picking, and watering without my help. "See, everything is fine, Nich. We got you," Jayden reminds me.

As we head for the highway and pass over the bridge to Long Island, I think about my future and where the next part of my journey will lead. What if I don't do well in my horticulture courses? What if I can't find a job? But like a sign from Papi, I hear his voice in my mind again and picture him smiling down on me: *Stop. Enjoy your life and focus on the present.*

I sigh in content and wrap my arm around Jayden's shoulders. No matter what happens, as long as I have my best friend, partner, family, and Cheese, I know everything will be perfect.

# AUTHOR'S NOTE

Thank you for taking the time to read this novel. This work was inspired by my personal journey with fibromyalgia, an autoimmune disease I was diagnosed with five years ago after experiencing multiple traumatic events in 2019. Fibromyalgia is a disease that takes away your freedom, just like Nichi experiences. There are some days you wake up perfectly fine while others feel like the worst flu. Your entire body aches, sometimes burns, and flares are often accompanied by nausea, loss of appetite, and extreme fatigue. Like Nichi, I often push past the pain when I really want to do something, like gardening and connecting with nature. Sometimes, there are consequences to this, like feeling major flu-like pain later, sometimes for days or even weeks! But to see a garden flourish after all that hard work is worth it. This year in 2024, I was also diagnosed with chronic migraines. It's safe to say writing this year was difficult, but I'm so glad to finally share this work with you.

A majority of the characters are inspired by loved ones who either supported or hindered my journey with fibromyalgia. Nichi represents a lot of the confusing thoughts with my own identity as a Latina. I don't speak fluent Spanish, nor do I have the beautiful caramel skin of my family, but that doesn't make me any less Nuyorican. Growing up in a Latin household meant I was raised by a strict mother, but there was also fierce love in her protective ways. Family gatherings like the ones in *Nuestro Corazones* were a regular event for holidays, but due to distance, this has faded away. Even though my family lives in a different state, I love cooking traditional Puerto Rican food with a vegetarian twist!

Another aspect of Nichi's life is her spirituality. Like me, Nichi walks the Neopagan path, meaning she worships Gaia instead of Dios(God) and nature. Neopaganism is a flexible spirituality, something Nichi and myself needed in the darkest times. Neopaganism is often portrayed as dark or evil in current media, but that's far from the truth. I encourage you to research this spirituality and its nuanced practice.

Finally, I want to thank all my readers, family, friends, and especially my beta readers, for constantly supporting my writing journey. It means so much to see your awesome reviews and shares on social media!

*Te quiero* and Blessed Be.
Kyla Stan

# THE SKIN WALKER SERIES BOOK 1

**She threw herself away – and was reborn as a alpha werewolf with a prophecy.**

Seventeen-year-old Violet Ashton is labeled as a Goth girl and secretly desires to find her purpose in a metal band. She wants a real connection, but her boyfriend Jake would rather party and thinks love is a joke. Trying to navigate through her senior year of high school while dealing with emotional abuse and bullies finally wears Violet down, and she believes everyone would be better off if she were dead. Fleeing society's brutal ways, she tries to kill herself by cutting her wrists.

Tohon, the gorgeous warrior son of a prominent Skin Walker chief, a race of beings that shapeshift into wolves, is expected to one day succeed his father and find the perfect mate to spend his life with. But Tohon breaks the ultimate Skin Walker rule: stay away from humans. When Tohon smells Violet's blood and saves her from committing suicide, he accidently bites her, forever marking her as a wolf and awakening an ancient prophecy. Violet has the power to destroy the enemy hunting Tohon's pack – but only if she is willing to risk her life.

Leading the greatest war in Skin Walker history is only part of the problem. Violet must also face long-buried issues of trust as her feelings for Tohon become something more than she ever expected. Is Violet a raging animal, or a gentle spirit? And can she face down the greatest enemy she has ever known in order to have the things she wants the most?

*Filled with Native American romance, mythology and paranormal fantasy elements, Poet Tongue is the first novel of the Skin Walker Series.*

# FORBIDDEN TIDES: A DARK YA MERMAID ROMANCE

*A Dark YA Romance with a science fiction twist!*

**Some would say I look like a mermaid, the essence of nautical beauty. I looked in the mirror and saw a monster....**

Astrid Murphy, born with strange webbed hands and a thirst for saltwater, feels like a freak. She desires to look and feel normal, just like her family. But Astrid doesn't realize that she's meant to be the next ruler of the Deep Clan, a race of merfolk who are dying from pollution and overhunting. She is the only one who can save them.

Zander's mission was to find Astrid and bring her home. Not fall in love with his target. Surrounded in a web of danger, a forbidden love between clan daughter and warrior blossoms. Zander knows they can't focus on each other, and the Deep Clan must come first. But it's the one enemy Astrid never expected who will tear it all down. Her father. The one person who was supposed to love and protect her, will do anything to keep her from fulfilling her destiny with Zander. Even kill.

As Astrid and Zander fight for their world, they learn the true depth of what it means to love, the power of hope, and what it means to be free.

## STAY CONNECTED WITH THE AUTHOR!

Make sure to sign up for my newsletter to receive exclusive release dates, fun giveaways, and other important events! Plus, you will instantly get 5 FREE chapters of *Forbidden Tides + Poet Tongue*!

Please go to KylaStanYABooks.com for more information. My website also has YA book reviews that discuss literary techniques and what future authors can learn from each book!

Follow me on Instagram @kylastanyaauthor and on Facebook @KStanYAAuthor for writing discussions, upcoming cover releases, and fun sewing projects that I create in my spare time.

Made in United States
North Haven, CT
28 January 2025